Losing Dominion

A novel by Mark McLean

Artwork by John Dunbar McLean
Cover design by Lindsay Vermeulen
lindsay_vermeulen@hotmail.com
Third Edition

For John and Maud McLean, and Andrew and Doris Sharp.

To my sons —

I don't think you've ever seen me drink, have you? Forgive me, I'm drunk now. I happen to have a nice bottle of scotch stored away for emergencies, which I open from time to time — one of the invaluable tips I learned from Dr. Beringer. Oh hell, you won't know who he is. Ask your mother.

The bottle's empty now, and I'm decidedly drunk. And what an occasion to drink. For the second time in my life I have lost a father, and now that my brother and sister have left the house, all I feel is an overwhelming need to talk to you. God, I don't know if I did right by you three.

The scotch was helpful but it wasn't enough. Stewart showed up soon after dinner and then my bottle emptied pretty quickly. Thank God your aunt brought in the cavalry, and the empty bottle was replaced with a full one. It didn't do much good. I mean, the scotch worked — the fact that I'm writing this at all testifies to that — but really it didn't do much good. It didn't console us. We just sat in the dining room, drunk, silent, hearing that damned clock tick away in the corner.

"I can't believe he's dead," was the only thing your aunt Grace could mutter all night.

"Pass the scotch," was all that your uncle Stewart could say, several times.

I kept pace and tried not to weep.

I hope I did right by all of you. I must seem as strange a man to you as your great-uncle was. I'll take the blame for that. I've watched you grow into men and make your own decisions, absolutely terrified that I somehow screwed things up for all of you. I've had trouble articulating my thoughts my entire life.

Grace was always far braver than me. I doubt I'll ever have the courage to say things like this to any of you in person. What a coward I am. Just like your grandfather.

I have never done anything more important in my life than provide for you. I spent every day fighting back the thought that I wasn't doing enough. Forgive me.

-Undated letter found while cataloguing James' estate.

I

My uncle Percy passed away three weeks ago. He came to visit the family for the Easter weekend, and died in his sleep in my brother's guest bedroom. He lived to be a ripe eighty-nine years. Despite his old age, the death came as a shock to the entire family: we've been waiting for his wife, Alice, to pass away. So when I heard Stewart's tone of voice over the phone, I assumed my aunt had finally succumbed to her cancer, and I must admit with a degree of relief. I didn't expect Percy.

My brother Stewart, my sister Grace, and I were left in charge of the will, and on a quiet Saturday morning we wandered through the old Toronto house, not looking for anything in particular but assessing and breathing in the remnants of Percy's life. The living room was quiet and still. The huge window overlooking the driveway let the daylight stream in, and the sun warmed the beautiful red rug that covered most of the hardwood floor. The walls were adorned with paintings of tall, green forests and dark, still lakes. Many of them were my wife's, and I wondered how we would divide them all between Stewart, Grace, and me. Percy didn't have many possessions, but neither my siblings nor I were looking forward to dividing his estate.

The basement held his small office, simply furnished, where he would retreat from Alice and the rest of the world. I thumbed through the account books and folders, looking for nothing in particular. In the top drawer of his desk I found a stapled document, with the title "The Life and Times of Percy McCrae." It was underneath a stack of tax receipts, as if he'd written it and placed it there as an afterthought. His autobiography (if we'd like to call it that) was only six pages long, filled with concise facts about his life, his family, and his various business deals. At no point did he seem to reflect upon the magnitude of any of his decisions.

After I read through it, I leaned back in Percy's old, weathered chair and stared at the title. I couldn't believe it. I felt a deep sadness that this great paternal figure thought his life could be sheepishly summarized on six pages. I smiled, though. This was quintessential Percy: the man who quietly provided without obligation for his bully of a wife, as well as three children who weren't his own, shrugged off his life in a memo. I grinned and showed Stewart and Grace when I walked back upstairs. They read through the pages, then scoffed and smiled as I did.

"I can't believe this is all he wrote," Grace whispered after she read it, the thin document still in her hands.

"Come on," replied Stewart. "I'm surprised he wrote anything at all."

We spent the rest of the afternoon in our own separate parts of the house, touching the furniture and listening to the creaks of the old home before we had to begin cataloguing. Stewart and Grace spent most of their time in their old rooms, while I looked through the garage with all its knickknacks. We agreed to meet again later in the week, to visit Alice at the hospital.

That night I had tea with my eldest son, Theodore, and told him about Percy's memoir. He was taken aback, and was tight lipped. He thought it sad, he said, as if a great opportunity had been missed. He seemed distracted for the remainder of the evening. After he left, I reluctantly drew up the paperwork for the estate. What a terrible thing, to wade through bureaucracy when all I wanted to do was mourn.

The next Sunday Theodore called, as he always does. After he met his wife, my son's interest in strengthening family relationships intensified, as if he felt a personal duty to bear some paternal responsibility. I enjoyed the change, and I could expect his call like clockwork. This time, we spoke mostly of Percy. He knew little about this quiet old man, who popped in and out of our lives between trips and hikes to nowhere. He told me that the memoir I found had been on his mind, and that it made him feel unsettled. I asked him why, but he had difficulty answering. My eldest has never been fond of confrontation, nor anything that had the potential to cause displeasure. He is a peace-at-all-costs man, which he doubtlessly inherited from me. I suppose he was hesitant to offend me in some way.

"I don't know, Dad. Since Rose was born I keep thinking about what it's like to be a father. You kind of get thrust into it, you know? Even if you plan ahead. I keep thinking about how you and Mom raised three boys, and I realize that I don't know a lot about you when you were my age."

Hmm.

My wife and I have been a constant presence in our children's lives, yet it had not occurred to my son until recently that I must have once lived for myself; growing up, one pays little attention to the history and sacrifices of their parents. I am not a talkative man – I leave that to my wife and my sister – and when it comes to the subject of me, I feel reluctant to speak at all. I have rarely spoken of my life before the births of my children to anyone. My son knows nothing about my time out west when I was younger, and he's never asked, but now he wants me to document it. He wants to make sure I don't end up a simple scrap of paper. Maybe what he really wants is to know where he came from.

He asked if I would consider writing an autobiography, a thorough one. I told him that I'd think about it.

*

It really is a monumental task. To pick and choose the stories of my life and document them for future generations is a heavy responsibility, and a time-consuming undertaking.

Two days ago I decided to do it. I am growing older and my family is growing larger. What happened in Vancouver altered my life and altered my country, and led me to my wife. My children deserve to know where they came from, though I'm not entirely sure how to begin.

My wife has become surprisingly vocal in support of the idea since it was raised. We rarely speak about that time in our lives, and I suppose three decades is enough time to allow this to remain unuttered. Though, now that I think of it, I've never been much of a writer. I've started journals from time to time, inspired by events in my boys' lives, but my writings fizzled with the monotony of days. This feels strange but comfortable.

*

When I was twenty-three, I was accepted into medical school at the University of Manitoba, in Winnipeg. I had no particular attachment to the city, nor did I have any family there, nor even a desire to be anywhere near the prairies. The only redeeming quality of Winnipeg was that it was closer to my family in Toronto than Vancouver was. Now that I stop to remember it, I was also accepted to the University of Alberta, though I decided to decline because of some unsavoury politics that the news had been reporting on campus. Apart from that, as most who went through the process of applying to Canadian medical schools will tell you, once you've been accepted, you go regardless of location, and Winnipeg had opened the door for me. Besides, being a doctor was far more important to me than where I spent my schooling for a few years.

So I went.

When I received the acceptance letter to the U of M, I was living in Vancouver, an undergraduate of the University of British Columbia,

Faculty of Science. I stayed in British Columbia to go to school when my family – my uncle Percy, my aunt Alice, my brother Stewart, and my sister Grace – moved to southern Ontario, the year after I got my high school diploma. I studied biochemistry for the most part, and excelled at it. My four years of undergraduate university were enjoyable enough, but I didn't like being away from the support of my family. I was not interested in a social life, and I did not try to make any friends. I was not an unpleasant fellow (I was kind enough); I just got along well on my own, and was happier for it. That doesn't mean that I didn't miss the company of my family, though. Because of my isolation, and my concentration on studies, there's not much to tell about the first three years of my degree – I worked diligently and interacted rarely. My final year, when I was sprinting to finish my thesis on time, is the only period of note, and that is where I'll start. It's the year I met Sarah.

*

Thus far I've been writing these first few passages on my back porch, sitting in a deep, wooden patio chair. There's a warm breeze right now. It's a peaceful process that's bringing to mind many things I'd forgotten, memories rushing to the foreground in waves that I'm struggling to organize. I'm fortunate enough that I have the pleasure of looking over the backyard while I do it. The garden is a recent project of mine in retirement, and I've enjoyed the patient process of watching plants grow from the dirt I turned. Now it's the beginning of summer – I feel the mugginess of Southern Ontario coming on. I created a section for the cucumbers, baby tomatoes and zucchinis, which will hopefully be part of our dinners, and another for the Black-eyed Susans and tulips that colour my vision. When spring started, I planned ahead for what to do this year, strolling through the yard as the late Toronto snow thawed around my marble birdbath. It is the centerpiece of what would be my garden, and its dirty water attracts the blue jays and robins in the morning. It's a charming way to wake up, with the chatter and splashing of birds. My youngest son gave me the birdbath for my 55th birthday. I can't remember a present of which I thought so little at the time and from which I have gained so much since. I don't understand where he got his foresight, but it wasn't from me. I never told him how much I appreciate his gift.

*

I wasn't born in British Columbia. When I was eight years old, I moved to Vancouver with Stewart and Grace by train. We came to live with my aunt Alice and uncle Percy on the North Shore, after my mother passed away in our home just north of Calgary. The memories I have of my youth are blurs of colours and smells and isolated images, and I see them like faded Kodaks, yellowed with age. What I now know about that time is a mixture of my own memories and bits of conversations with Percy and Alice. I've never taken a great interest in rediscovering my childhood; it is not in my mind an important piece of who I am, other than that certain events led me to Vancouver.

When I was a baby, my father and his sister Alice received a significant inheritance after their parents' deaths. He used his to buy a large plot of country north of Calgary and settle down with his wife (I only know this because I overheard Alice and Percy speak). I don't know why he bought the land, perhaps he had an inclination for farming. Alice chose to invest in the house that I would eventually live in. I remember little of the Alberta home, other than snapshots of dirt and dead grass, and rolling hills.

What I remember of my father is that he was a happy man. Looking back, I know that he was shunned by the family because of his wife, though I've never known the reason. It is perhaps because of this that he isolated his wife and children to the farmlands of Alberta, though that can only be speculation. I think he accepted his status without bitterness, however; any memory of my father is connected with warmth and confidence. From what I recall, I had a happy childhood.

My mother died in childbirth. My sister Grace came into the world as my mother left, and I recall loud cries coming from our home in the middle of the stretching prairies. Stewart and I were playing outside the house, and listened as we heard an adult scream turn into a child's scream, and then both were silent. I heard my father yell "NO!", followed by a crashing sound from within. The last memory of my father is of him leaning his head against the front doorway, crying. I had never seen a man cry. I watched him and didn't know what to do, not understanding what had happened. He walked back in the house, and soon the midwife came out and told us about our new baby sister. I never saw him again.

How could a child possibly understand the complexity of what had happened? I can't remember how I felt, though I can only imagine that I was confused about the turn of events. I don't know when my father left the house, but for the next three days he was gone, and the midwife took care of Stewart and I, and the newborn Grace. I don't remember who she was, but she must have been a formidable woman; I have no doubt that Grace would not have survived without her presence. On the fourth day Alice showed up at the front door. I had met her once before, and I knew she was my father's sister. She told us that she was taking us away, that daddy was very sick, and that we were going to see the ocean.

The next memory I have is of the train. It swayed gently from side to side, as my eight-year-old self watched Calgary, and my childhood, slip away behind me. Soon we were taking a steady pace through the mountains, imposing giants I'd only seen on clear days from my isolated home.

We took up two rows of seats facing each other. Stewart slept with his mouth open, drool dangling from the corner. Alice sat across from me, cradling the sleeping Grace, and stared straight through me. I hurt my neck, craning to see the peaks of the closest mountains. I could not comprehend what awesome forces could pull these great slabs of earth upright. I was frightened at all the changes happening around me, but I soon fell asleep like Stewart. Alice's eyes were alert, almost angry, fixed on something beyond the walls of the train.

*

In my fourth and final year of university I was living in East Vancouver, alone in a cramped studio apartment. It was tucked away near Main and Broadway, an area known for trendy cafés and counterculture clothing stores. I was neither trendy nor countercultured, but I liked the atmosphere, and I wanted to stay close to campus while avoiding Kitsilano – too many pregnant people. I took a liking to the café Bean Around the World: a clean, somewhat somber place, rarely too busy. When I wasn't in class I could usually be found there, studying or reading in solitude, working to complete my Honours thesis. I didn't like being in my apartment any more than I had to: I didn't know the steps to make it into a home, so I became familiar enough with public locations that they became my home. Besides my one particular coffee shop, where the employees were used to my presence, I had a deep affection for the Central Library downtown.

It was at the café that I met Sarah. She was a regular, though not to the same degree as I was, and she smiled and waved at me whenever we saw one another there. Shy, I'd smile and nod back. Before long, she strolled up and introduced herself.

"So you're science, eh?" She said, eyeing the sprawling textbooks on my table.

Yes, I said, and looked uncomfortably back at her. When she realized that I wasn't going to say anything else, she went on.

"Arts, myself. Well, social work, actually. But Arts too."

Great, I said. I held my pen in the writing position, unsure of how long this conversation would last. An awkward moment passed, because she didn't know that I was not planning on fulfilling my small-talk duties. She figured it out, though.

"So I see you here often enough that I thought, well, maybe we should study together?" She raised her eyebrows hopefully.

Um, sure. Why don't you pull up a chair? She did, and we exchanged names. My palms got sweaty.

"Pleased to meet you."

Likewise.

After this we worked on our own respective assignments, and she left well before I did.

"See you next time," she smiled. I nodded back. When she was gone I breathed deeply and sighed, thinking something like: *What the hell was that?*

But true to her word, we were studying together the next day. From then on, whenever we happened to be in the café at the same time, which really was whenever she happened to drop in, we studied at the same table. I made it very clear that my time was for studying, and we got on well, speaking rarely. And that's how I began an actual friendship.

*

Yesterday my brother and I went to see Alice at the hospital. We drove in my car, and I told him that I was writing a book, at Theodore's request.

"Theo's really becoming a man," he said.

Yes, he certainly is, I replied as I felt a blooming pride. We stayed silent awhile longer.

"How are his younger siblings?" Stewart turned to me.

Far away. I replied, as we pulled into the parking lot. We made our way to Alice's room.

She was barely conscious, and in rough shape: her face was locked in bitterness and she spat swear words to no one in particular. She has not been lucid enough for her to understand that her husband of sixty years is dead. She muttered a few things about him, as well as commonplace concerns about the home, and I knew she was thinking of 45 Perkly, not the family home in Toronto. She never stopped feeling that that was her home, years after the move to Ontario. There were moments of lucidity when she understood we were in the room, but she still didn't recognize us. We didn't stay very long, and I drove Stewart to his house afterwards. I came in briefly to say hello to his wife, then returned home to have dinner with mine. I've spent enough time with my siblings and sister-in-law lately because of the estate. I felt weary and wanted to go home.

*

My entire final year of undergrad, Sarah's presence at the café was a constant, and she was really the only friend I had while in university. I was really not a social person. Without my family, I led a pretty isolated life, and was content to do so. Sarah never pushed me, and seemed to understand my desire for solitude. From time to time she would come in the café with a friend, would wave at me, and then sit at another table. I was grateful for this, since I don't meet new people well, and she never imposed anyone else upon me. If her friends left before her, she would silently come join me for the rest of her time there. I liked her being around. She seemed to understand that I didn't want to talk while I studied, and that my academics were more of a priority than enjoying the pleasure of her company.

In fact, one of the few times I initiated a conversation with Sarah was to tell her that I was accepted into medical school at the University of Manitoba. She was genuinely happy for me, nodding her head and smiling warmly. She tucked her hair behind her ears, then spoke.

"Oh, wait a second. I know," she said, then abruptly stood up. Her chair scraped along the hardwood floor. She spoke to the employee behind the counter – a young, bearded fellow who smiled and nodded. She gave him a blue five-dollar bill, and he gave her a slice of chocolate cake. When he thanked her by name, I realized that Sarah seemed to know everyone. She brought me the cake.

What's this?

"Well, it's a congratulatory cake, so eat up. Yum!" She said this while rubbing her belly, hoping to transfer her excitement to me.

This is a bit of a change from my normal coffee and biscotti, I smiled, picking up the fork. *Are you going to help?*

Sarah kind of jumped in her seat. "Oh, right." Everything she said seemed to be reinforced with an effusive energy. She wasn't tacky or loud; she just seemed to be excited about most things. She dug in.

Something changed after that, and we spoke more often. I don't know why she kept coming back to the café to study with me – I'm a dreadful conversationalist. Yet she was there regularly, and it became the high point of my day to see her come in through the front doors. It had been four years since I'd had consistent company, and I hadn't noticed how lonely I'd become. I did go on dates sporadically in university, like I had in high school, usually with confident women who mistook my shyness for depth. My relationship with Sarah was something of a different variety. Her presence was reassuring, even if our conversations were superficial.

When the school year wound down, and I found myself facing four months without reason to come to the café, Sarah and I agreed to spend time together outside of our usual rendezvous.

"You sure you're ready for this?" she asked with a playful, worried face.

What?

"Our entire friendship," then she covered her mouth in shock and whispered *friendship* as though it were a scandal, "is based on books and caffeine. I don't know if we can handle the sun."

Well I guess we'll just figure it out.

She smiled, and we took each other's numbers.

*

Alice, Stewart, Grace and I pulled up to our new house in the cab. We had waved it down at the train station, and the ride into the city seemed otherworldly. To get to the house on the North Shore, we drove through downtown Vancouver. I saw buildings soaring up to the sky and people milling about on sidewalks. I saw bright colours and shiny windows and marvelous fountains. I never knew of such places. We drove through Stanley Park, and I marveled at the thick trees and lush green of everything around me. It was as if some slumbering, benevolent creature inhabited those woods and protected it. We drove over the Lions Gate Bridge, and I saw the glittering ocean for the first time in my life. It separated Vancouver from the North Shore municipalities like a great moat. We drove up a steep hill and turned onto Perkly Road.

The driveway was gravel, and wound in a loose, steep 'S' through a copse of trees to reveal what would become my home. It was an elegant, simple house. A golden 45 adorned the door. From its perch surrounded by trees, it had a breathtaking view of the city, and its facade was dominated by a large living room window. Stewart and I carried the luggage from the cab up to the front door, and Alice held Grace in her arms.

I first met Percy as I entered 45 Perkly. We walked in, and Percy walked out. He carried a worn down canvas bag over his shoulder, and was dressed in jeans and a plaid shirt. He was surprised to see us, as if he had hoped to leave before we arrived, so he muttered a gruff 'hello', threw his bag in the back of his truck, and started his engine. Alice glared at him over the baby. We didn't see him again for a week.

Alice led us into our new home. The place was immaculate. It was furnished comfortably, and it felt like a home, but it was the type of clean where visitors understand immediately that messes are not tolerated. Stewart and I stood in the front hallway, mouths agape at the palace before us. Life before that had been dirty floors and clutter everywhere.

Stewart and I had our own separate rooms, though his was smaller – a fact for which he would begrudge me the rest of our lives. Grace stayed in Alice and Percy's room, down the hall from the entrance. The front door opened into a tidy living room, with a couch and coffee table, a china cabinet, and a dining table. Behind a low ledge was the kitchen, well equipped and well organized. All the bedrooms were on the main floor. The house seemed gigantic to us.

We settled in, and got used to the routine. Stewart and I have always been on the quiet side, with the brief exception of Stewart's political stint with puberty – it was Grace who would fill the conversational gap in later years. We did what we were told without complaint. Life under Alice was an adjustment. We learned that she was stern but usually fair, and had a sharp tongue if we stepped out of line. Percy, when he was home, was rarely seen. For the most part, he kept to his study where he worked on whatever it is civil engineers work on.

Grace greeted me at her apartment door this morning with her usual childlike grin. Her presence is always a calming force for me: the fact that she remains so young at heart after all these years is like a breath of fresh air. She makes me feel like an older brother.

She has a fine apartment. On the outskirts of downtown Toronto, it is cozy, modest, and well thought-out. I've assumed that because she never married, she was able to spend her money, which would otherwise go towards a family, on the aesthetics of her living space. Her walls are adorned with family pictures, not only of her brothers and their children, but also of distant relatives I'd long ago given up staying in contact with; relationships always functioned with ease for Grace.

Today is a day off in her sporadic nursing schedule, and we enjoyed a slow-paced, high-calorie meal she whipped up all on her own. I've often wondered why she, as such a personable woman, never ended up with anyone; perhaps it is her quirky nature. She seems far more relaxed with Alice out of the apartment and in the hospital, and I told her so.

"It is nice," she smiled through half-chewed toast. She bought fresh, delicious multigrain loaves from a local bakery. I could see guilt tug at her lips as she swallowed her bite. "The hospital is so well equipped for terminal patients. I guess you know that. But it's nice to go and be a visitor. See her properly taken care of. Irony is, I guess, she has no idea of the care she's getting. Funny, cause if she knew what the hell was going on anyway, she'd hate being doted on, you know? Oh, I don't know," she shoveled some sausages in her mouth and looked upwards. "Can't tell if she even recognizes us anymore. More tea?"

Yes, thank you. She barely knew we were there, when Stewart and I visited.

She nodded over her cup of chocolate milk. "Yeah, that's how she is pretty much all the time now. Poor Alice." She munched her heavily buttered toast.

Sarah and I met regularly over the summer. She lived in the northern edge of downtown with some roommates from university, and I lived in East Van – about twenty minutes by bus. Instead of going to the other's apartment, we'd meet somewhere in the middle and explore the city on foot. Once a week we met up and walked Vancouver's streets, drinking coffee and talking (though she spoke more than I). She got to know the city as well as I already did.

I showed her my favourite spots in the Central Library, and we'd walk around its perimeter, marveling at such a grand monument to learning. She took me down Robson Street and tried to educate me on everything retail. We stopped in stores and tried on clothes, and I was bewildered. She told me what clothes to buy and I bought them, but I didn't know the difference. I usually just enjoyed watching the crowds go by around us in a hurry, and the wafts of fried onions from the hot dog stands. I took her around the north side of Stanley Park's Sea Wall and pointed out where my old home was, hidden somewhere in the trees of the mountainside, across the inlet. The moment I pointed it out I felt homesick.

She took me to Queen Elizabeth Park, which had a beautiful panorama of the city. Long ago it was a volcano, and is now the highest point in Vancouver. It had well-tended greenery and weaving paths through the trees: a fine place, I would discover later, for a walk at night. We explored a new place every time we met, right until the week before I left for Winnipeg. The last time we met that summer, we sat on a bench along Cambie Bridge, looking northwest at the other bridges. They carried streams of cars in and out of downtown. The apartment buildings looked like turrets protecting against invaders. It was my favourite view of the city.

I'll miss you, you know.

She gave me a little check with her shoulder. "What is this, feelings camp?"

I grunted.

"Yeah, I'll miss you too. But you know," she said, and put her arm around my shoulders, "now you'll have to come back and visit me."

Hmm. I nodded my head. We sat like that until sunset, then I hugged her goodbye and we went separate directions. I caught my flight the next day, and said farewell to the city of my youth.

*

My wife wakes up before me every day except Sunday. She likes the quiet of the morning, when she can work in peace. She'll sit in her studio, upright on her stool, and look out the window at the swaying trees for several minutes. I can only imagine what she thinks of in those moments. Without a prompt she'll begin painting, laying the groundwork for what's to come. I don't understand the foresight of her works. There's some meticulous planning that happens in her head, and her ability is beyond me. She stops at lunch and I can see the beginning of a structured vista, some lake or forest that only she can see.

She asks me, while we eat some cold roast beef sandwiches, how my writing goes.

Good, I mutter, and she nods.

She's been quiet about my writing, and though she is supportive as she always is, I can feel her apprehension.

She's gone back to her painting.

*

Moving to Winnipeg for medical school was no small feat. Vancouver is a temperate city, and I had lived there for most of my life. I knew the difference between winter and summer as a juxtaposition of chilly temperatures in overcast skies or sunny days with warm weather, but nothing drastic that ever altered my lifestyle. The entire city screamed moderation, and this is what I was accustomed to, along with a backdrop of beautiful mountains. I was not prepared for the extremes of Winnipeg, where my calm summers were replaced by oppressive heat and violent thunderstorms, and my damp winters by thick snow and biting cold. Winnipeggers are proud of their climatic hardiness, and they are right to be so. But it took me some time to understand why people wanted to live there at all.

My earliest memory of the city was of leaving the Winnipeg airport in mid-August. Inside, the air conditioning was cold enough for a sweater. Stepping outside, after the automatic sliding doors cut off the supply of fresh air, the humidity settled on my skin and in my lungs. Prairie heat is often overlooked in discussions about Manitoba weather, since the cold is so astounding, yet it is no less formidable. I remember staring at the sidewalk from the shade, the blinding bright glare coming off the concrete.

I took a cab, and watched the handful of Winnipeg's downtown buildings jut unimpressively out of the middle of the city. The apartment I had found to stay in was a hole. There was one small bedroom with one small bed, right next to a poorly lit and aged bathroom. The kitchen worked well enough, and it shared a space with the living room. I had a two-person couch in front of a small coffee table, where I could rest my feet while watching the old television set that came with the apartment. The living room window looked over the street below, from my lofty second floor view. The campus and the downtown core (such as it was) were pretty easily accessible by the bus, when it showed up.

*

Before we moved into their house, Percy and Alice lived their lives assuming that they would never have children. In fact, there have been some indications that their marriage had never been consummated, let alone carry the possibility of offspring. Their house was, therefore, thoroughly unprepared for an onslaught of youth. While Alice had her hands full tending for Grace, Stewart and I explored our new territory.

The house was quiet except for the steady tick of a grandfather clock in the living room. Everything was pristine, yet innately warm; as if Alice kept it just so, not to please visitors, but to calm her own sense of order. Stewart and I learned to tiptoe around certain parts of the house: the china cabinet, the sound system, and anywhere Alice was at that particular moment. Though all the bedrooms were upstairs, we eventually claimed the lesser-used basement as our play area. There we stayed for hours with our toys, dutifully returning everything after we finished. It did not seem to bother Percy, who worked in his office the next room over. I don't know if we were naturally good children, or if I'm projecting our present personalities onto our younger selves, but we were careful not to encroach too much on our aunt and uncle's hospitality. For a long time we feared that they would get rid of us.

We became familiar with our surroundings. Outside, 45 Perkly was fenced in closely with trees behind and around it, and the front yard dropped down into more woods about fifteen meters from the front door, so the driveway up was on quite an incline. We played a lot in the trees, since we were used to being outdoors during the day. While I could see its beauty from almost anywhere on the property, I had little initial interest in the distant city of Vancouver.

*

My first year in medical school was rewarding academically, but physically stressful. I excelled, as I resumed a rigorous study schedule that my classmates had to learn from scratch. By the end of the year I was comfortably top of the class, and had developed a reputation as a professional, if quiet, gentleman – an image that stayed with me throughout my career. I spoke on the phone regularly with Percy and Alice, and Grace kept a charming habit of sending me letters, which got very eccentric as she progressed through puberty. Sarah and I kept in touch, though the regularity of our contact that year was determined by our school schedules (she was finishing her undergraduate degree), and we sometimes went weeks without hearing from each other.

I had trouble adjusting to Winnipeg. The first winter the weather was so bad that I feared leaving the house. When I left before dawn to catch the bus to school, I made certain that there was no exposed skin except for my eyes. Even with all my layers I felt a deep chill for much of the day. I learned that back-up pairs of socks were a blessing, and long johns were no shame at all; indeed, they meant the difference between a good day and a bad day. I felt cabin fever, along with the rest of the city, since I refused to spend any more time outside than was absolutely necessary.

I made no friends, which by this point in my life was not much of a surprise. While my study habits and my personality ensured this, I found people in the city difficult to befriend. Their reputation for being warm and personable is well deserved. It was a rare day that I was not saluted by a stranger, or saw acts of kindness occur between people who did not know each other. But across the board I found a reluctance to make new friends. Childhood friends in Winnipeg remain friends for life. This created tight-knit and trusting groups, and it also made new members rare. With my reluctance to start conversations, friendships weren't likely. I was not yet accustomed to the city by the end of my first year.

*

Theodore brought my only grandchild Rose over this morning. She's two years old now and is showing all the signs of a tyrannical childhood – plus she has her father wrapped tightly around her little finger. Perhaps this is an old man's wishful thought, but she and I have a special relationship. She listens to me, most of the time, and loves showing off when I'm around. The latest thing for her has been demonstrating how well she jumps, from the first step of the stairs to the floor. She'll stand on the step, crouch, stumble to the floor and land on her butt, then kick her legs in the air and giggle. Then she'll to it again. And again. I watched her while I drank tea, and smiled every time she looked over for approval. She farted loudly at one point when she crouched for a new jump. This came as a surprise to her, and she brought her hands up to her mouth and giggled. I snorted so hard that my tea spilled over the lip of my cup.

*

By the time I finished my first year of medical school, Grace – fourteen years old and fifteen hundred kilometers away in Ontario – was in the full swing of puberty, and had become a nuisance to her aunt and uncle. She was insistent on returning to Vancouver for a visit to see the friends she left behind, and I volunteered to meet her in the Winnipeg airport for her connecting flight to Vancouver, and board the plane. I chaperoned for a week.

We stayed at Jade's empty house – she was one of Alice's old bridge partners, and was kind enough to leave her house for us while she was off on her summer vacation. Being back in Vancouver was absolutely rejuvenating. It was good to breathe that air and see those mountains again. Grace spent much of her time sprinting between friends' houses, sleeping over. I was largely left alone, hardly an effective supervisor. I was happy to take the city by myself, though, and I enjoyed a respite where I had no choice but to read for leisure and watch television. In hindsight there weren't any shows that I watched religiously, and that was the week that the sovereigntists swept into power in Alberta, so the news covered little else – all week there were clips of protests and pundits, as the country tried to grasp what this meant for the elusive Canadian identity. I took little interest at the time, but nothing else was on. Still, it was nice to have something on in the background. So I stayed most nights at the house and read from the selections on their bookshelves. I contemplated going to visit 45 Perkly. It felt like a gravitational tug everywhere I went, but I decided against it; some other family lived there now. Besides, Vancouver was no longer my home, and I suppose I interpreted such desires as childish.

I called up Sarah and we took several outings together, to new locations in the city. We walked, as we always did. My heart warmed seeing her, and she seemed grateful to have me back in the city. We compared our year apart, and I congratulated her on having been accepted to a master's program at Simon Fraser University, one she decided to defer for another year to save some money. She couldn't believe that anyone could live in such a cold place as the Canadian prairies. I found myself strangely protective of Winnipeg, and mumbled half-hearted defenses. Grace wanted to meet this one friend that I seemed to have, and so we arranged to spend the day at the Vancouver Aquarium. They got along well, though Grace was distracted by her fluorescent surroundings, as well as whatever thoughts flitted about in her pubescent brain. We said goodbye to Sarah once we all returned downtown, then Grace and I transferred to another bus.

"She's cute," was the first thing that came out of her mouth.

Shut up, I told her and nudged her. She responded with something like "ooo", and then went on to tell me about the latest in pop culture. We left the next day – I on a flight to Winnipeg, she on a flight to Toronto. In hindsight, that was the last time I would ever see the Aquarium.

*

Once Grace was out of her infancy and was able to crawl about, Alice returned to her old routine around the house. Her old routine was new to us, since we only knew her in the capacity of caring for our baby sister. She spent several hours a day cleaning the house and reading her book in intervals, and spent the rest of the time preparing meals. She went about this with unwavering dedication, and rarely left the house. I always imagined that she was displeased with the outside world, and did not wish to endorse it by being in its midst. She allowed herself one weekly indulgence: every Tuesday night, she invited her friends over to play a game of bridge. Stewart and I, who had just become accustomed to life in the home, had to readjust to this new schedule. We walked on eggshells when she was around, but it was an inevitability that we would feel the wrath of Alice.

In one instance, I was being chased around the house by Stewart. We were boys: we played. At the time, Alice normally took a nap. I can't imagine what forces roused her from her sleep, but she was regrettably not in bed and, rounding a corner, I bumped into her. She fell back into the china cabinet. It wobbled precariously. We both stared at it, as the dark wood teetered and the precious dishes trembled. Nothing fell, but her eyes fell on me with anger once it settled. Her fear for the safety of the china drove her to punish me. Stewart, the coward, was nowhere in sight when she gave me a thorough spanking. I'd never felt such humiliation in my life, and I cried when she sent me to my room. I berated myself. I had been so careful not to upset my new host, and here I had gone and almost done damage to her and her property. That stung far more than my bright red behind. Though she never spoke to me about it afterwards, I recall her giving me dessert first that night. Normally Percy ate first, under the pretense that he had a great deal of work to do and had to hurry. This might have just as well meant nothing, though. I didn't talk to Stewart for days.

He had his turn, a month later. It was a Tuesday, one of her bridge nights. Her friends attended with such regularity that I remember their names to this day: Betsy, Jade and Baba. Baba's actually name was Dorothy. I don't know why they called her that. They were loud, feisty women, who enjoyed their liquor and loudly proclaimed their opinions. It was the only time that Alice seemed happy.

Stewart, perhaps seeking to tap into her good mood, offered to cater their drinks one Tuesday. Alice agreed with the wave of her hand, and her friends squealed with pleasure at the sight of this seven-year-old carrying martinis on a silver tray. He soon spilt one of the drinks on Baba's lap. The game stopped as she sprung to her feet, and kindly smiled, wiping the wet spot on her skirt. I watched from the kitchen.

"Oh, it's alright," she proclaimed loudly. "I never liked this skirt anyways." Betsy and Jade laughed with her, but Alice sat quietly. She stared at Stewart with a look we would come to recognize as very bad news. She rose curtly and whispered, "I'm very sorry about this, Baba." She took Stewart's hand and dragged him to his room. The entire house could hear her thunderous yelling. Their bridge game resumed after Alice slammed Stewart's door shut, and the laughter that accompanied it swelled again. Stewart did not come out until morning. I laid low in my own room.

She was a hard woman, and Stewart and I did our best to stay out of her way. We didn't want to inconvenience her, or in any way make her regret her decision to take us in. We never begrudged her. In her way she loved us and tried to protect us, though it was rarely evident. She could be forgiven for lacking the parenting skills necessary to look after three children, when she never planned to have them.

*

My impression of Winnipeg changed in my second year at the university. I was more prepared for the rigours of winter, and though I still had few friends, the consistency of my presence at some places brought warm greetings from those who recognized me. I grew comfortable, and fell in love, quite unexpectedly, with the subtlety of prairie life.

One night I stood before the front window of my apartment, which looked out over the street below. A soft snow was falling, and I made a cup of tea and turned out the lights. Outside, the snow fell beneath the light of a single streetlamp. It was as if the snow simply appeared in the soft yellow triangle and drifted gently to the ground, just for me. I felt such peace. The next morning when I set out of the house, there was no wind and the sun had not yet risen. The snow crunched beneath every one of my steps. It made me smile.

The winter was starting to grow on me.

*

Sunday mornings my wife and I rise early and get ready for church. We have an old routine: I wake up fifteen minutes before her to put on coffee and make toast, and we have breakfast in silence before getting dressed. The trade-off for me waking earlier than her is that after the service she bakes oatmeal chocolate chip cookies, and the last spoonful of raw cookie dough is reserved for me. Of course, most of the leftover cookies go to our granddaughter. I'm spoiled and prefer them fresh from the oven.

Lately, something odd has been happening. This morning I turned my alarm clock off and blinked in the early sunlight. Three windows let the light stream in, which brightens the room. Strangely, my wife was already awake. She stared at the ceiling, like a child unsure of what to do next and awaiting instructions. When I kissed her forehead, she blinked in confusion and smiled at me. She whispered that she was going to sleep for another ten minutes, and then rolled over.

Her cookies today were soft and gooey. I grimaced when she pried some away from me to give to Rose.

*

After the winter, my second year passed quickly. Ever since I visited Vancouver, Sarah had been far more consistent in her emails and phone calls, and she planned a visit for the next summer. For the only time in my life, I would have to play tour guide in Winnipeg.

She came in early August and slept on the couch. I was happy to see her, but relieved that she only stayed for a weekend: I don't host well, and I doubt my company would have been pleasant much longer. For the time she was there, though, we enjoyed ourselves. I took her to the tourist sites that I had not been to. We took the bus heading to the Forks, and she asked me where downtown was. When I pointed out the five or so buildings sitting squat in the distance, she said: "Oh, isn't that cute?"

The Forks was my favourite part of Winnipeg. Right next to downtown, it's the heart of culture in the city. It reminded me of Vancouver's Granville Island, though Vancouver lacks the richness of history that Winnipeg boasts. I showed her what remained of Upper Fort Garry: a single wall from the fort that protected Manitoba in its infancy, and housed Louis Riel before he fled the Canadian forces. Most of it was torn down to make way for Main Street. Sarah adored this one monument to Winnipeg's modern history, tucked away downtown, almost unnoticeable and covered with graffiti.

This is where Manitoba was born, I told her.

She nodded absent-mindedly and smiled in appreciation for the graffiti, which I actually thought had defaced a national treasure. We left, walked down Portage in the dusty heat until sunset, and then got on a bus and headed home. She flew back to Vancouver on a Sunday night, and our long-distance friendship resumed into my third year at the University of Manitoba and her first as a Master's student.

*

A rhythm developed at 45 Perkly, as Stewart and I became accustomed to life in school. Though he and I have always been pretty reserved, he finds friends with far greater ease than I; throughout school he fit in comfortably and quietly, while I was pretty well left alone, and happy for it. I spent much of my youth studying and doing homework at school and at home. When I grew old enough to leave the house on my own, I took to studying in cafés and libraries. Though I had a deep fondness for the shelter of 45 Perkly, I liked the solitude of anonymity away from the family. It felt like an assertion of independence. I also had trouble being in the same place as Alice all the time. Her bitter snaps at Percy and her woeful concerns about money were a daily occurrence, and I did all that I could to avoid them. Every action Percy took seemed to elicit some negative response from his wife. It didn't take long for me to understand why Percy was always away on some business or hiking trip. Only his private office in the basement seemed to be an area of truce between he and Alice, otherwise she would snap at him for evidence of any money spent that wasn't strictly necessary. I have no doubt that he regretted his marriage.

*

The final two years of medical school flew by. The second half of a medical degree is mostly rotations, or clerkships, where students get hands-on experience in a wide variety of fields. I spent most of my rotations at the Saint Boniface Hospital in Winnipeg. My third year was consumed with all the mandatory experiences that the university ordained, and so I was exposed to all types of medicine. It was stressful. I learned to sleep whenever the opportunity presented itself, and eat whenever food was around. There's a pecking order at every hospital, and we all had to start at the bottom of the rung. It was an eye-opening year, a pressure cooker where the twenty-four months of previous knowledge had to remold itself quickly to be easily accessible. Being a medical student on rotations means being quick on your feet or drowning, and there was little recognition, and no recompense. My fourth year was a relief: I got to choose more of my courses, and make my education based far more on internal medicine. I knew that it limited my options for the future to concentrate so heavily in one field, but I was steadfast in my desire to be a family doctor. The two years went by quickly. Before I had time to reflect, it was soon time to graduate.

Sarah and I called each other often and regularly during this time. I became…affectionate towards her. She was the first person outside of my family whom I had ever cared for, and this frightened me. I visited her again, one weekend in my third summer and we walked along the entire Seawall – quite a long stroll. We had plenty to talk about, between her Master's thesis and my hospital experiences, and she was someone whom I trusted enough to confide my thoughts in. I became accustomed to the regularity of her calls, and of knowing what was going on in her life. She dated from time to time, and I surprised myself with pangs of jealousy. At the time I didn't know how to deal with such emotions properly, so I ignored them.

We both looked forward to completing our respective degrees, which happened to finish at the same time. For me, it was the end of my formal education – after this, I would be a practicing doctor, even if a lowly resident. I had finally reached my goal. For her, it was another step in her evolving concept of what she wanted to become.

*

Neither Stewart nor I had ever been to church before moving to Vancouver. Perhaps my father was an atheist, or maybe he was just apathetic. Whatever the reason, I never gave much thought to religion until I met Alice. She was a devout Anglican, and insisted that we accompany her every Sunday. By some inconceivable arrangement, Percy was never expected to come with us.

I accepted religion, as most children do, and I have fond memories of our old church. The priest was a kind, middle-aged woman, who joked with the congregation. In hindsight, it was quite an informal atmosphere, and it avoided much of the rigidity that churches burden themselves with. I understood little of what was taught, but I liked the sense of community, shy as I was. I remember the bland, dry taste of the communion wafers as a necessary first step to get to the wine, which tasted fantastic and strange. I recall the stained glass windows with melancholic figures staring off, and the smell of dust balls and disinfectant. It was a place of peace.

*

Most of my rotations were a blur of small tasks and exhausting days. I recall one patient well though: he was an older man, black hair graying gracefully, who had the misfortune of being a bystander in a clash between demonstrators downtown. The secessionists had just been declared the losers by a slight margin in the Albertan referendum. Each side accused the other of tampering, and all across Western Canada, sympathy protests had sprung up. The man I treated happened to be walking down Broadway when the two groups of protesters went at each other, and he got a shard of glass in the abdomen. It was not a serious injury, but it required stitches, which I administered.

"Thanks kid," he muttered, and smiled at me as I started the stitches.

Don't worry about it.

"Can you believe this crap?" I smiled and nodded. "I mean the protests. I can't believe it. Never thought I'd see the day when people out here would get so worked up."

I know.

"I mean, I know a lot of people were pissed off back when Trudeau was in charge, but nothing like this. Who are these people?"

I gave a half grin as I concentrated. *I don't know. My little brother got into it for a while there. The family didn't put up with that for long.*

"No kidding...how long?"

'Bout a minute.

The man laughed. "I don't know how it all got to this."

Well, I said as I finished up, *I'm sure it'll die down soon enough.*

Then he said what makes me remember him at all: "Now listen, kid. You're probably not old enough to remember what happened in Quebec, but these things can escalate quickly. Watch out for your brother, okay?"

I looked at him for a moment. *I will. Thank you.* I walked out of them room.

Stewart, of course, never really flirted too heavily with secessionism. Once, around dinnertime, the subject of the growing movement came up, as something that was discussed at school. What Stewart said was: "I don't see why we're spending so much money keeping people around who want to go. Let them leave if they want."

"You mind your tongue!" Alice chewed him out pretty good for that statement, and I never heard him bring it up again.

*

Today I met Stewart at his house for a cup of tea and some estate work. He lives in Oakville, a suburb of Toronto, and when I arrived, he welcomed me in at the front door before I'd even walked up the steps. Stewart has a dry hospitality, and has since the birth of his first child (much like my first son, now that I think of it). He tends to greet me gruffly as if I'm a minor nuisance in his schedule, though I know he loays forward to anything with the family. The house was empty for the afternoon, since his wife took the grandkids to the mall. Though it was only he and I, his house, as it always seems, was warm and inviting, as if its occupants had only just left and will return with freshly baked goods for company. I consider this more a testament to his wife, considering how cheap I know my brother can be. They bought the house soon after they married, and it has accumulated styles from three generations of furniture, art, and decorations. The rooms were all darker than I prefer, but they created an eccentric and very cozy environment. He and his wife recently paid off the entire place, something he is very proud of – as he should be.

Documents were spread out over the living room table, and we spent the afternoon sorting through some of the final papers for Percy's estate. Our families had already gone through his possessions with few hitches, and all that remained was putting the house on the market and tying up a few loose ends. We worked quietly over the paperwork on his living room table. I drank a cup of tea, he a reheated coffee.

We talked about Alice. Everyone has become so used to the fact that she was dying, even considering the recent death of Percy, that it was really just a waiting game. She is getting rapidly worse now, and the cancer has spread to a point where she clearly has little time left. We decided to ask Grace whether she thought it would be appropriate to bring Alice into one of our homes for her final days, or whether we should leave her under the care of the hospital. By dinnertime all the papers that needed signing were signed, and we put the house on the market.

*

I flew into Vancouver to celebrate the coincidence of my graduation from medical school with Sarah's completion of her Master's thesis. A friend of hers contacted me some weeks before, inviting me to come celebrate with her entire group. We agreed to keep it a secret from Sarah. I landed on a Saturday evening dressed in my best, or what Sarah once told me was my best, with only a backpack; my flight out of town was the next afternoon, since I had an interview with Winnipeg's Saint Boniface hospital on Monday morning. I took the Canada Line downtown, to the Yaletown stop, where her friend had told me they'd be.

The celebrations, strangely enough, were taking place at a bar underneath the Central Library. I guess they thought it fitting, as if their one last hurrah with academia should be a drunken stupor beneath a mountain of books. By the time I got there a line had formed outside the bar, and so I waited. It seemed absurd to fly across half a continent only to wait meters from a door, meters from Sarah, but there was really nothing I could do, so I stood there shuffling my feet. Sarah's friend was not answering my calls.

When I finally got in, I saw Sarah dancing on the floor with her friends, her hair swinging about. She was a sight to see when she let loose, and it occurred to me then that I had never seen her drunk. I went to the bar and ordered myself a beer, then made my way towards her.

Hi, I yelled over her shoulder.

She screamed and jumped in the air. She saw me, then screamed again and launched herself into a flying hug. She was grinning when she let go.

"What the fuck are you doing here?"

Don't worry about it. Congratulations!

"Thanks, thanks. Shit, you too! Holy fuck, what are you doing here?" She gave me a punch on the arm. I think she was tipsy.

I danced awkwardly with her for a while, then we went to sit down. The whole night was up and down between our table and the dance floor, and Sarah easily outpaced me in drinks.

Something was different in the way she acted that night. Whether it was the alcohol, the sudden release from responsibility, or the company of her friends, she was definitely flirtatious. When she spoke to me she leaned in and I felt her breath on my ear and my neck, and she would place her hand on my leg, or my arm, or my chest. I felt butterflies at her touch. She pulled her hand away several times and apologized. She kept telling me that it was important that I not read into anything she was doing. She was clearly drunk by the time the night wound down and we all left the bar.

Outside the library, her friends started smoking. Sarah, who didn't smoke (nor did I at the time), took me aside and put her arms around my waist. She looked up at me and smiled.

"You're here," she whispered.

Yes, I know.

She leaned up and kissed me. Her lips were soft and wet, and smaller than mine.

I kissed back; I was surprised, and didn't know how else to respond. We parted and she smiled contentedly.

"I've liked you for so long you know," she muttered, and rested her head against my chest. I didn't know what to say, so I didn't say anything. My mind was racing. At that moment her friends loudly came around the corner, and she and I broke apart. The group decided to call it a night, and sorted out who was going in what direction. Sarah was looking straight at me, but I avoided her gaze and nodded when her friend asked if I was still crashing on her couch. Her friend and I took a cab home in silence, and I found myself overwhelmed with an intense longing for Sarah and a reluctance to act. I did not sleep well that night.

I woke the next morning and changed for my flight from the clothes in my backpack. I thanked Sarah's friend for her hospitality, and asked to use her computer before I left.

I had a single message, from Sarah.

Hey,

I'm so sorry about last night. That was completely inappropriate. Frankly I'm too embarrassed to call. Please tell me that we're still friends.

I'm glad I got to see you.

Sarah

I closed the window on her computer and headed out the front door. I didn't want to reply because I had no idea how to respond. I felt emotions pull me in directions I had never known, and it seemed prudent to turn it over in my head on the flight back to Winnipeg. I didn't message her until late that evening.

Hello, sorry for the delay. Don't worry about it, of course we're still friends. I'll call you soon, okay?

Truth was, the plane trip didn't make it any clearer for me. My feelings were a jumbled mess. I'd never had such strong feelings for anyone before, and I didn't know whether my emotions justified jeopardizing the only friendship I had. I'm certain that my delay in response was hurtful.

Stewart and I enjoyed Alice's bridge nights immensely, despite past reprimands. We knew to stay out of her way – neither of us volunteered to help with the drinks again, or anything for that matter. We liked those nights because it was the only time that Alice seemed happy, or at least not surly. She rode whatever happiness she experienced that night into the next day, and Wednesdays were always the most pleasant day of the week. Our lunches on Wednesdays were more ornate, and often contained a candy bar. Even Percy emerged from his den most Wednesday nights to watch television for a while, comfortable in the assumption that Alice wouldn't snap at him about doing something better with his time. Wednesdays were my favourite day.

For me, I enjoyed peeking in on the games. Stewart was forever terrified after that one day when Alice hosted, so he mostly kept to himself and read quietly in his room. Percy, similarly, took extra precautions to avoid being seen on those nights. The one time he made an accidental appearance, returning home from a trip in the middle of a game, Alice raised her glass as if to toast him.

"My idiot husband shows his face!" She said, and I could see her friends cringe. "Back from yet another little expedition? Where did you go this time, dear?" Percy looked down and walked past me in the hallway, heading downstairs to his office. Thereafter, he made sure to time his returns better.

I discovered that if I stood in the hallways around the corner, I could listen and peak in from time to time, and scurry into the bathroom when anyone headed to the kitchen. I most enjoyed inspecting what was happening when the adults went into the kitchen. I didn't understand the elaborate ceremony put into making martini drinks, but I watched it with interest. Between games, Alice and Baba would go to the kitchen together to make another round of drinks, and I remember Alice smiling the whole time as she whispered excitedly to her friend. Once, I saw Baba lean in and mutter something in Alice's ear, who leaned back and barked a laugh. I'd never seen her laugh before. She placed her hand on the small of Baba's back as she brought the drinks out on a tray, and Baba followed her laughing. I was happy that Alice had such a friend, even if I was somewhat resentful of how she treated Percy. It was like seeing who she really was for one night a week, and the remaining days were a façade.

*

I got the residency position at Saint Boniface Hospital in Winnipeg. The job started in September, so it was an easy enough process for me to extend the rent at my terrible apartment.

Sarah and I resumed our friendship and never spoke of the night outside the library, but it hovered behind everything we said to one another. I'm sure that she was terrified to bring it up again because of my silence, and I was immobilized by uncertainty and cowardice. I had feelings for her, but I couldn't decide how strong those feelings were, or if they merited a long-distance relationship. I had never had a girlfriend before. This was uncharted territory for me, and I had no idea what to do. I hid behind my indecision, and she suffered for it. We kept a regular correspondence when I started work in the hospital, and she carried on with life by the ocean.

The time I spent in Saint Boniface was an incredible learning experience. Medical school certainly taught me what I needed for the job, but the new weight of responsibility made it all the more sobering. I came to better learn the pace and demands of a hospital and, exhausted, I felt validated in my choice of profession. During rotations, med school students are fledglings in coping mode, and though the entire experience is overwhelming, all that is learned are the bare necessities of being a doctor. They work under residents who work under attendants who work under, who work under. So when I was finally able to enter the workforce, I got fantastic exposure to actual medicine and greater responsibility. It was even more time-consuming than rotations, but I had the advantage of being young and single, with a penchant for isolation. While I was there, my residency was very successful.

*

I watched my wife paint today. Rather, I snuck glances at what she was doing as I read from a book – she doesn't like being watched while she paints. She's been working on a beautiful vista, an image that I recognize. It's based off of a photo I took while on a hike by Muskoka Lake. A serene pond lies in the foreground, while green trees, fallen and standing, populate the background. In the middle is the vibrant red of a tree hurrying to autumn. It leans over the pond, ripples of crimson reflecting in the waters below.

*

The city of Winnipeg is surrounded by a roughly circular highway, called The Perimeter. The great debate in Winnipeg is whether it takes less time to take the Perimeter around the city at 100 kmh (faster than that really, because few police cars patrol it, and they can be seen from miles away) or within the city at 60 kmh. I had purchased a second-hand car in my third year, which I justified as being necessary for the clerkship section of my degree, and was very helpful while on call during any residency. It was an old Volvo, and it was reliable when I needed it. Whenever I got stressed or overwhelmed, as I was in the weeks after I last saw Sarah, I took to the Perimeter and circled the city for as long as I needed, weaving past the slower cars and staring at the urban sprawl snuggling up against the highway. I loved the vast prairie sky and the endless land; I felt exposed and raw, naked before the rest of the world. I must have circled around Winnipeg dozens of times, before that car suddenly became very important to me.

I was in the hospital cafeteria when I first heard about the earthquake in Vancouver. The huge room had gleaming white tiles that reflected the cheap fluorescent lighting above, and long collapsible tables stretching from the counter to the windows. An entire wall was glass, and I remember that a sunset was setting the sky afire. I was eating alone with my tray, in the corner by myself. A few other people, mostly family of patients, were quietly nibbling on whatever they bought. I heard the clicking of heels. A doctor walked by the entrance, hesitated, then came in and spoke.

"I don't know if any of you've heard yet, but Vancouver's been hit with an earthquake. There's a TV in the lounge if you want to watch." She walked out.

I stared at the empty doorframe for a moment, then dropped my spoon. It clattered off the table and onto the tiled floor. All at once everyone in the room got up and headed for the nearest television they could find. We crowded into the waiting room, where a small television hung from the corner ceiling. The room was filled with family members and nurses. The station was tuned to CBC.

The headline underneath the images read: BREAKING NEWS: MAJOR EARTHQUAKE HITS VANCOUVER. I felt my gut sink. The only clip they showed at the time was from a few minutes earlier. A young female reporter was speaking with a middle-aged man when the camera started to shake violently. The two ducked and screamed as sounds of rumbling and crashing broke out around them, then the feed was lost. I suppose this was the only shot they had at the time, because they played it over and over again.

People walked into the waiting area in search of news while others walked out to find loved ones. A regular stream of anxious people came in with open mouths and wide eyes. I didn't report back to work after dinner, but they didn't seem to care. I sat there and watched the video continue in a loop, while the anchors hypothesized.

I took out my cell phone and dialed the number that burned in my brain. Busy signal. Every time a busy signal. I felt nauseous.

All of Canada stopped that day to watch Vancouver crumble. Images and video started streaming in and were broadcast immediately. They showed clips from convenience store security cameras – shelves swaying back and forth and toppling over. They showed videos from reporters who were already in the area, depicting flattened homes and buildings on fire and people screaming as they watched the destruction of their livelihood. The earthquake was a catastrophe, and the early images showed the chaos of the immediate aftermath. I stared at the screen for hours listening to a busy signal, and looked for Sarah among the mourners. She was somewhere there, and I couldn't find out what had happened to her. I kept thinking about her kiss outside the library. I felt shame burn through me.

By late evening the Prime Minister addressed the country, urging calm and promising immediate aid to the area. He took no questions, and within the hour other party leaders pledged in sequence to work together to help the people of British Columbia.

The countries of the world poured in condolences and contributions. America could be forgiven for worrying about the earthquake's effects on their side of the border. At the time, they were having just as much trouble keeping their country together as we were. They had their own problems to deal with.

A group of doctors at St. Boniface registered the next morning to go to Vancouver. The federal government was organizing it, and I signed up, despite my inexperience, as soon as I heard that it existed. It was never a question. Vancouver was my home. 45 Perkly was there, even if its occupants had changed. Sarah was there.

The Premier of Manitoba urged any and all immediate assistance from her constituents. Most of the provinces were lining up to help as well, by sending medical staff and engineers. Alberta and Quebec had their hands full with their own separatist politics, and couldn't send as many. Immediately protests broke out in those provinces, as secessionists warned against exploiting this tragedy in the name of federalism. Ironically, those provinces were among the most generous in per-capita private donations to the Red Cross. Every province contributed something and waited on the federal government's next move.

I gave up trying to call Sarah; cell phones were down all across the region, and there was no way to reach her. I called Percy and Alice – they were as worried as I was. Alice was near hysterical, and could barely be understood. Their friends were there, just as Grace's and Stewart's were, and they could not be contacted. Alice was beside herself. I told them that I was joining the doctors heading west. Alice didn't like it at all and told me so: she thought it was far too dangerous. Percy just told me to be safe, and that they'll help in any way they can. I told them I'd contact them before I left. I don't think they knew about Sarah – in their minds, this was probably all about a duty to serve.

More news came. It was all bad. The earthquake was the one Vancouver had expected for a long time, yet there's little to be done to prepare for something like that. Houses and skyscrapers alike had crumbled or were too dangerous to approach; shards of glass covered downtown streets, making them completely inaccessible; landslides had swept through parts of the North Shore. There was no safe drinking water, and no electricity to boil it. It was a worst-case scenario.

The city and the province declared a state of emergency. They didn't have the resources or the manpower to deal with the enormity of what had happened, and so they knocked loudly on Ottawa's door. At the time, the federal government sensed an historic opportunity to restore not only Vancouver, but an entire country, to its former greatness.

*

Still in elementary school, I got to know Alice's closest friend Baba as a kind and sassy woman. When Stewart and I were too young to leave the house by ourselves too often, she was our link to the outside world. We never knew her husband growing up, but we knew he was wealthy, and she didn't have to work a day in her life. She had a sharp tongue and a quick wit, and she would burst with laughter when we made good points against some of the stories she told. We liked her. Her laughter wasn't patronizing. It was joyful, as if inside she was laughing all the time and only needed an excuse to let it out. The stories she told us were mythical in proportion, from parties she frequented to news she heard; she made everything sound wonderful and scandalous, and she always looked as if she were stealing something from the cookie jar. She lived large. Her presence drastically altered the energy of our quiet, ordered home.

She and Alice were very close. Percy's absence was a constant through much of our youth, and I think Baba was the only person Alice felt she could confide in. They whispered on the couch over cups of tea often enough that it became quite normal, as if Baba were a member of the household. They were close companions. Perhaps what I loved most about her was that she always carried candy in her purse. Mints and Werther's. Alice frowned upon excesses of any kind, so Baba would hurriedly wave us over when Alice was out of the room, and slip a handful of candies into our outstretched fingers. She'd then shush us, and pat our bums to scurry us away. We were devastated when she stopped coming to the house.

*

Careers have been established in trying to explain what happened in Ottawa that year, as well as its effects on Canada and the rest of the world. The political tensions beforehand aren't always addressed in attempts to explain what happened; documentaries and history books tend to focus on the aftermath of that one late January afternoon. I'll repeat it because the events directly affected the course of my life, not because I have anything new to say. This is how I remember it.

Canada's government had been yanked in several directions at once by its own citizens for several years, and Parliament became a political nightmare. It had been quite some time since any party controlled a majority of the seats in the Lower Chamber. In a string of minority governments, Prime Ministers rose and fell as the opposition parties ganged up to defeat them. Power went back and forth between three federalist parties, none of them ever gaining much of a mandate from elections. The three relied on two separatist parties for survival, each one prone to the whims of political fortunes. Every alliance was short-lived. A year before the earthquake, riding a wave of populist support from provincial elections and referendums, a Western Canadian separatist party gained a chunk of Alberta federal ridings, which split the right-wing base and let the moderates squeak in with a very weak minority. So Parliament had three national parties that wanted to keep the country together but distrusted one another, and two separatist parties – one from the west and one from Quebec – with whom nobody could deal publicly, because their goal was to split Canada apart. The situation was messy, to say the least. Another election, which nobody wanted, was likely around the corner.

The emergency in British Columbia provided a rallying point for federalist parties, despite the protests: they saw it as a chance to unite Canada behind a common goal. The Prime Minister emerged from a meeting with the leader of the Opposition, and they declared an historic, if temporary, coalition to pass a series of bills aimed at restoring Vancouver as a world-class city, and at keeping Canada together. Together they created an emergency plan for Vancouver. For a time, there was hope that this would work.

The media trumpeted the coalition as an exciting experiment, the possible saving grace of Canada; the mature thing to do, as all Canadians gathered together to support Vancouver. The leaders of the separatist parties ranted on national television. They claimed to sympathize for the people of Vancouver, but warned against overreaching federalism. Ominously, they predicted a surge in public violence against federal institutions. They received little sympathy. Though some fringe separatist groups were vocal and sometimes destructive elements in larger protests, we hadn't yet seen a return to the days of the FLQ, where terrorism was used as a political tool in Canada.

In late January, not three days after the earthquake, Parliament set up a vote to send financial aid to British Columbia and to pass a series of bills that would ensure Vancouver's long-term recovery. Every MP came to vote for this, the trumpeting of a new political era, regardless of the party they represented.

*

For my entire youth, Alice did little to elicit sympathy. There was one notable exception. In the late spring of my first year at 45 Perkly, I walked up the driveway to find Baba's car idling in front of the house. I knocked on the window, which she rolled down in surprise. She had been crying, and dabbed her eyes with a tissue.

Hey Baba.

"Hey kid. Just coming home from school?" She smiled to hide her sadness, but mascara had run down her face.

Yes ma'am. Is everything okay? I felt very uncomfortable.

"Yeah, yeah. I was just leaving. I'll see you soon, okay?" She put the car in reverse and backed up slowly down the driveway, winding out of sight beyond the trees. I stared after her for a while. I was afraid to go into the house.

Eventually I eased the front door open and slung off my backpack. Once I removed my shoes, I tiptoed into the living room. I heard something coming from Alice and Percy's bedroom. Slowly I walked towards it. Their door was open a crack.

Alice was lying on the bed, her back turned to me. She was crying. Her hands covered her face, and her body shook with each breath. A box of tissues lay on the bed in front of her, while some used ones sat on the nightstand.

I moved slightly and saw that Percy was sitting on the bed next to her. He was silent, and watched her cry. His hand rubbed her back slowly. I stood, watching this tender scene, when Percy turned his head and saw me looking in. I was terrified that I had overstepped my bounds, that I was looking in on something I wasn't supposed to see. Children shouldn't see grownups cry.

Percy rose and walked to the door. He stood there, looking at me with searching eyes. Then he smiled warmly at me. I felt suddenly reassured. I think he wanted to convey that I had done nothing wrong by seeing what I saw. I felt safe with that look on his face. His smile turned into a soft, neutral look, and he closed the door.

*

The morning came when the team of doctors was to leave for Vancouver, and I was at home packing a suitcase in the living room, with the television on. Outside, the sun was climbing up in the sky, and it shone through my living room window. I watched the news to kill the time until I had to leave. CBC was covering the budget vote scheduled that morning, and made a great deal of fanfare about the coalition. These were two natural enemies joining for the good of the country. Word was that they had already mixed the cabinet equally between them. The separatist parties had toned down their rhetoric against the budget, because of regional sympathy for Vancouver, but still grumbled about the shackles of federalism infringing on the rights of provinces. From what I remember, people didn't much care about what the politicians were saying. I finished my packing. I had time to watch the vote. The Members of Parliament had filled the chamber, all of them waiting for the Prime Minister to arrive.

I watched as the cameras followed him stepping out of his black car in front of Parliament. He stopped and waved a gloved hand to the crowd of people watching from the barricade across the lawn. You could see his breath rise in front of him. I'd never seen a Prime Minister walk in for a vote before. I suppose he wanted the symbolism: the man in charge humbly approaching Canada's democratic emblem. He walked through the front door of the building, and the cameras followed as the sound of an explosion ripped through the air. Debris sprayed from the door the Prime Minister had just walked through, the glass windows on either side of the entrance shattering out onto the lawn. A second later, the central part of the building exploded in a series of huge concussions and rising balls of flame.

I watched. I was filled with an unutterable awe, a wave of horror and excitement. The camera shook without control, and was knocked to the ground. I couldn't understand what had happened. I stood up in my living room and stared at my television. I willed it to explain. It said nothing, but screamed screams like those from Vancouver I'd heard for three days already.

The image that is now well known, that of the Peace Tower collapsing backwards into the building, wasn't actually shown on television until the next day, when the press began showing reruns of different angles. Someone told me that. I didn't watch a lot of television for the next little while.

No one claimed responsibility that day, nor any day since, but in the various witch-hunts thereafter the finger has often been pointed at zealous separatist groups. They had been prone to small-scale violence, but never anything on this scale. I don't think it really matters, at this point.

Every federally elected representative died that day. Every one. Admirable or not, each started with the intent of making their world somehow better, and felt safe in a peaceful society. They traveled from across a vast country to cast a single vote, to save a beautiful city on the edge of the world. Not one of them survived.

*

My book came up for discussion at dinner tonight. I doubt I'll ever comfortably talk about my past to my family, but speaking about this is cathartic: I feel a growing anxiety about it. The book has become something I feel is important, that I need to finish.

My second son David brought his husband Edward to dinner. It's rare that they're both in town, and I convinced Theodore to join us with his wife and daughter. All day I looked forward to seeing my two sons and their spouses.

Their mother cooked roast beef with potatoes, mashed squash and garlic bread. Rose munched on Wheat Thins, taken from a nearby silver canister that I keep well stocked just for her. I steered the conversation initially, and we discussed the state of my son-in-law's firm, the progress of my granddaughter, and the beauty of the back garden. Inevitably, my wife started playing devil's advocate with our children. This is what they do, despite my best efforts: they bicker. They argue about everything and somehow enjoy it. Between volleys I tried to ask my children-in-law polite questions. As is always the case, I gave in and listened to my family fight. I felt a familiar amused frustration at their dinnertime antics. This is how evening meals have passed in our family since our boys could talk.

The smell of roasted potatoes in the blood of rare beef, the pleasure of emptied and refilled glasses of red wine, and the familiarity of conversation that resonates with decades of memory and practice, all made me smile to myself. It filled me with a bittersweet aching. I miss having all of my three sons under one roof.

*

The expedition of doctors to Vancouver was cancelled in the aftermath of the explosion. People were shocked, justifiably terrified. Every federally elected official had just died, and it was not at all clear who was in charge, or indeed if anyone was in charge. In Winnipeg calm was largely kept, though people made a run on grocery stores and bottled water. Without direction from Ottawa, help to Vancouver sputtered and stalled immediately, and my convoy of doctors dissipated without the guidance of a centralized government.

For the rest of the day I sat and stared at the television, trying to find Sarah somewhere in the back and forth clips of Ottawa and Vancouver. For a full day I watched as my life began to rip apart, and as the country I knew and loved spiraled out of control. Still I tried to call her, and still no result.

After a day and night of restless pacing in my tiny apartment, I packed everything I cared to keep, and headed for the bank at dawn. I withdrew six thousand dollars, effectively emptying my account, and stuffed the envelope into the glove box of my car. I pulled up to a Safeway and stocked up on whatever canned food and candy bars were left. There were no more bottles of water, so I emptied several two-liters of cola and filled them with tap water from the bathroom. I packed everything in the trunk. I filled up on gas at the nearby station, breathed in the sharp cold, and watched the meter climb. I topped it off, got in the car, and idled. I took out my cell phone and called Sarah's number one more time. Busy signal. I called Percy, and got his message machine. I told him that I was going to Vancouver, with or without other doctors, then powered down the phone.

From the parking lot of a Winnipeg gas station, in the dead of the prairie winter, I pulled onto the road and headed for Vancouver on the Canadian highway.

II

I passed the Perimeter of Winnipeg by late morning. Highway 1 stretched out of sight before me, and I left the city as a ship leaves the port of an island. The land was vast and white, uninterrupted except for occasional groves of trees and isolated farmhouses. I hovered right above the speed limit. I wasn't sure what it was that I was doing, except that I needed to get to Vancouver. I drove without sound and without music, taking occasional sips from my water bottle, and watched the endless horizon approach with mesmerizing monotony.

The thick sheet of snow covering the fields made bare the eerie flatness of the prairies. In summer, fields of yellow mustard and wheat swayed in ripples spanning acres of land, providing a living painting to soothe the eyes as drivers stared passively ahead. Now the land was lifeless, and I clung to civilization on a straight black line stretching beyond vision, cushioned by heaps of plowed snow. This was the purgatory through which I traveled, without fully comprehending why.

The Canadian Highway stretches from the Atlantic to the Pacific like a spine, resting on top of the American border. Sometime past Winnipeg the road splits in two. One way heads northwest to Saskatoon, Edmonton, and northern British Columbia. The other heads straight west to Regina, Calgary, and Vancouver. I took the latter when it came time to choose, though I didn't know what I was going to do once I got to the end of it. I didn't know if Sarah was even alive, and if she was, I didn't know what I'd say to her.

Doubt crept into my thoughts. I'd never done a rash thing in my life, yet here I was, heading to a far off, dangerous environment with no clear goal and no clear plan. I suppose at the time the alternative – to stay in Winnipeg and do nothing – seemed unacceptable. I could see no other way to assuage my conscience and my turbulent emotions than to find Sarah the quickest way possible.

A few hours after I'd left the parking lot, I passed through a small town by the border of Manitoba. On the outskirts a hitchhiker stood against the gusts of cold wind next to a gas station. He was clad in an impressively large parka, with bushy fur rimming the hood. On an impulse I pulled the car over, and rolled down the passenger window. I leaned over in my seat.

Where're you headed?

"Small town north of Regina," he said.

I'm heading that way too. Come on in.

He slipped in and placed his rucksack between his feet, rubbed his hands together in front of the hot air coming from the dashboard, and muttered, "Thanks man". He pulled back his hoodie to reveal a long, straight black ponytail. "Nobody's stopping today."

I guess that makes sense.

He nodded.

We drove in silence for some time. I had never hitchhiked or picked up a hitchhiker before. I don't think I knew anyone who had even participated in the act at all, at least not by that point in my life. I didn't know the protocol. Do I speak first? Does he? What do we talk about? I was perfectly at peace to drive in silence on my own, but I've never been too familiar with the rules governing paired interactions. The drive from Winnipeg to Regina takes around six hours – about the amount of reliable hours of sunlight on a winter's day that far north. We weren't halfway there though, which made for a long time in silence. I decided to initiate a conversation, and so drew a deep breath.

So where exactly are you heading?

He looked at me quickly and shifted his body slightly, as if he felt physically compelled to acknowledge that it was talking time. It took him a minute to get out of his reverie. He cleared his throat.

"Um…sorry," he started. "It's a reserve north of Regina."

Oh okay. What's there?

"Home," he smiled.

Well that's good.

"Yup." He knew I was trying. "Where are you heading?"

I became immediately uncomfortable. I felt instinctively that if I uttered my plans they would shatter. *Past Regina*, I offered.

He nodded, and looked out the window.

So what were you doing away from home?

He let out a brisk sigh. "Working. My cousin helped me out with a job."

Oh? What line of work?

54

"Construction. Government contract. Lucky to get any kinda job like that in winter man. Had to leave though, hope he's not pissed."

Who?

"My cousin."

Right.

"Yeah."

Quiet settled in. I nervously gripped the steering wheel.

So why'd you leave work?

He grimaced. "All this shit out east man," he looked down at his feet. "I don't know. Felt right to go home."

Yeah, I muttered. I thought of 45 Perkly's front entrance.

"Where were you when it happened?"

Oh I was watching on TV when the explosion came. Watched the news coverage for the better part of a day before I took off.

"'Bout the same for me. It's crazy eh? Never seen anything like it. Shit, I knew I had to go as soon as it happened."

Why's that?

"Well a part of it all those damned cops I see around now, you know? After the attack, suddenly security is all beefed up. I mean, I know, it makes sense, but come on. This isn't Quebec, this isn't some campus in Alberta, this is the middle of nowhere. I see it out east and out west, but here? Here I feel like they're just looking for a boogieman. I didn't feel safe anymore. I knew I wouldn't feel safe anywhere but home. Time like this, I want to be around people I know."

How long have you been away from home?

"Too long. Got a girl waiting for me." He couldn't hide his smile.

Yeah, I smiled. I hadn't smiled in days. I don't think it was genuine, but it felt good to try.

He leaned his head back and sighed. "Yeah man. Her name is Ellia. I tricked her into dating me." He winked at me. "Been together ten years now, lived together for nine. Six months ago I walked into our kitchen, right, while she was making some bannock. Shit her bannock's good man. I can't wait. So I come in and see her gorgeous self cookin for us both," he motioned his hands to indicate her figure, "and I asked her if she wanted to marry me. She turned and winked. Fucking winked. She says, 'What's your hurry?'" He smiled. "I just want to be home, you know?"

I nodded.

He looked at me. "You got a girl?"

I don't know.

He nodded and looked out his window, lost in thought. We didn't speak much more beyond that until I dropped him off at a diner a couple hours later, just outside of Regina.

"Best of luck," he said as he left the car.

Yeah, you too.

I found a motel nearby and checked in for the night. The clerk gave me a room but only if I paid for the night in cash. I crashed onto the bed and dreamt anxious dreams I forgot the moment I woke.

*

I drove my second son David and his husband Edward to the airport. The mishmash of highways frustrates visitors and commuters in Toronto, but I have a fondness for the layout. Seeing the tiered freeways arching over one another and watching the lanes expand and contract fills me with a wonder at the eccentric foresight of city planning. It forces me to reflect that somewhere sometime ago, someone made decisions about what goes where, and this affects the path of individuals for centuries.

At the drop-off, I asked David whether he'd heard from his younger brother. Edward conspicuously slipped off to get some coffee at a glance from his husband. David put down his bag and sighed. He looked me in the eye.

"Yeah, Dad. I talked to Brian a few days ago online. He's in Japan right now."

Is he well?

"Yeah, I think so. I think he's trying to figure things out over there, you know?"

I nodded my head and shuffled my feet.

I wished them farewell, and hoped they would return soon. The chance to see them both is so rare these days. I drove home with a heavy heart.

*

I woke up to the winter sunrise in a quiet motel room. The bed was stiff and smelled of dust. I had slept fully dressed in my jeans and sweater, so I checked my pockets and put on my heavy coat. Brisk winter morning clears the senses. I looked at the sun with hands in my pockets – it was still cloudless, and my breath rose in a vapour. The car door was frosted over and took a good yank to open. Inside, everything my bare hands touched felt like ice. After warming the car up, I pulled out of the parking lot, heading west again on the Canadian highway.

For the rest of the day I drove in silence across the prairies. Two thin, unbroken black lines peeked out of the white road, where cars routinely passed over. Occasionally the wind would pick up, and wisps of snow would stream across the road like effervescent, playful snakes – broken, I'm sure, as I passed them. I saw few cars on the road.

I stopped that night just past the Alberta border. I dared not drive long after nightfall, because the snow that the sun had heated on the road would swiftly turn to slippery ice, wreaking havoc for travelers. Since it was winter, daylight hours were scarce. I didn't want to push my luck.

I stayed in a nicer hotel – this one had a gift shop – and wasted time there while waiting for the clerk to show up. The usual paraphernalia of the time was available: soft moose toys, maple candies and maple syrup, ugly shirts diagonally emblazoned with "Alberta!" across the chest, postcards proudly declaring the mosquito as the national bird. I saw a postcard of the Rocky Mountains, and stared at it until the clerk returned. He also demanded cash up front, which I provided easily.

Once in the room, I again lay on the bed fully clothed, staring at the ceiling in silence. The television was blank and I didn't want to turn it on. Finally I fell asleep.

The alarm clock went off at 5:45 the next morning. I recall this well because I had not set it, and was annoyed; the previous occupant must have forgotten to turn it off. I woke to the sound of the morning news: they announced a declaration by the Governor General from the day before, that he would enact his constitutional obligation and govern until the next election. His first priority, he said, was the security of Canadians. I turned it off; they wouldn't be telling me anything that mattered to me. I lay staring at the ceiling.

I didn't realize it then, but that was the first time I had been in Alberta since we left by train when I was eight.

A few years passed since the day I saw Alice cry. Stewart and I moved on to high school and Grace grew into an intelligible child. Percy was still rarely at home those years. He was either off working a contract or camping somewhere, but he seemed to spend incrementally more time at 45 Perkly, albeit tucked away in his office. I admired Percy the more I was around him. I decided that he had a good heart and an unfortunate lot in life, though I was too young and shy to initiate any conversation.

One summer day I got a call from one of the girls at school, who nervously asked me to join her at a movie that night. I heard girls giggling in the background. Invitations like this were sometimes extended to me, by my fifteenth year. I never understood why, since I hardly spoke at school. Perhaps they thought me handsome. I didn't see the point in being rude and saying no, but on this occasion I was short of cash. Percy was quietly working in his den, hoping not to be noticed, when I came and asked him for a twenty to go see a movie with someone. He stopped scribbling on some form and put down his pencil. He looked at me with a coy little smile. He knew I didn't have friends to go to the movies with.

As he pulled out his wallet from his back pocket, Alice passed by with a laundry basket and witnessed the sordid sight of freely given money. I had to scamper away as she burst into a fit of screams over wasted finances.

"What is this? How can you go about giving money away without consulting me? Maybe you should try spending more time doing something useful instead of running off every other week. Maybe then we'd have more money. Useless!" This went on.

Their argument, if you can call a monologue such a thing, lasted nearly ten minutes, and I took refuge at the upstairs living room table with a warm cup of tea. When it was finished, she stormed upstairs and took her anger out by cleaning the dishes. Five minutes later, Percy cautiously sloped into the room and sat next to me. His wife stared expectantly. Percy stared ahead and began, as if by memory:

"I hope you understand that I cannot give you any money. One of the lessons of growing up is learning how to appreciate the things already given to you. You understand?"

I nodded. It was the longest string of words I'd ever heard him say.

He rose and reached out his right hand, as if a deal amongst business partners had been formalized. I shook it, and he stumbled out of the room. Alice smiled in approval – her point was made. Below the table, I opened my hand and found a folded fifty-dollar bill.

The movie that night was charming. The company was not.

*

The radio address had triggered something in me. I was suddenly and profoundly aware that I had barely eaten in three days. I walked to the diner attached to the hotel, and took a seat at a table by the window. Cars occasionally passed by, all of them heading east. The only other patrons in the restaurant were a family of five. The father looked nervous and fidgety, and glanced about him as if searching for their waitress. The mother protectively watched her three children eat, ignoring the husband. As I ate my hefty breakfast, a man who was likely the owner came in and turned on the television. Everyone, even the children, stopped eating and watched.

The local news came on, discussing what was happening in Calgary. A dark man with a red and blue tie informed us that an exodus was occurring in Calgary and in every other major Canadian city, as families headed south to the American border. A backlog had formed for miles at several points across the country's border, presumably in response to the political instability, as Americans tried to return home or Canadians fled their own. In response to the crisis, the United States government shut its borders. They feared that the sudden influx of frightened refugees could cause too much chaos. Thousands of cars were now stranded on the cold Canadian highways.

Meanwhile, Vancouver reportedly was deteriorating as federal aid dried up, though information was difficult to come by. It appeared that looting and some rioting was taking place across the city. More was to come as the information rolled in.

"Turn the thing off dammit. You're scaring my kids." I couldn't see their faces from my angle, but the father's complaint was enough to make the owner comply. He paid his bill, and I left soon thereafter, leaving a green twenty on the table.

I backed out of the parking lot and headed for the highway. The road began to change. Here the land slowly rose and fell, like geologic waves rippling outwards from the mountains, moving too slowly to see. I was getting close.

I saw another hitchhiker on the side of the road once I passed Calgary. I hesitated, since I was eager to reach the mountains without delay. I acted on instinct. I pulled over and she climbed in, throwing her large bag into the backseat.

We greeted each other, and I asked her name.

"Anne," she said.

I told her I was pleased to meet her.

*

Since retirement, painting has been my wife's main hobby, just as I have concentrated on the back garden. For each of us, it's more than something to do; it's a peaceful, private sphere for us to inhabit individually. Time in isolation is invaluable to each of us.

In the past few months her art has grown more varied, even eccentrically diverse. Perhaps not diverse. Polarized. I'll check on her by midday and her canvas is covered with swirls of dark red over top of geometric black. The movements instill a brooding fear within me – she has never painted anything like that. Other days she'll wake and paint delightful, unstructured mosaics, of bright and varied colours. They were something one might see in passing at a children's hospital, placed to make a parent forget, for the briefest of moments, the horrible turmoil of their thoughts. Other days she returns to her classic depictions of nature. This happens less often now, despite the beautiful fall colours of our neighbourhood.

*

Neither Anne nor I spoke for some time, as Calgary receded in my rearview mirror.

I asked her where she was headed.

"West," she said.

I was quiet. I had the impression that she wasn't a talker. After deliberating about whether I wanted to encourage discussion, I decided to attempt a joke.

Never heard of that town.

She turned to look at me and raised an eyebrow. "Funny," she muttered.

We continued in silence. With the crest of each hill, the mountains grew larger in front of me. They were covered in snow, patches of grey rock peeking through.

Seriously, where're you headed.

She pursed her lips and said, "Vancouver."

That's bold.

She didn't respond.

Not many people heading that way.

"Nope."

Why do you want to go there?

She sighed and lightly rubbed her thumb over her heart.

Well?

"I'm looking for someone."

Who?

"Whom."

Okay whom?

She didn't answer, but looked north out of the passenger window. Ahead, the mountains loomed larger, and I began to feel exhilarated. They were gorgeous. They were an impending threshold, like passing into another world.

"Where are *you* heading?"

Sorry?

"Where are you heading?"

Vancouver.

"Why?"

Well I suppose that's not your business.

"Hmm."

She looked north.

"Mind if I hitch a ride for awhile?"

We're going the same place, no reason we can't drive the whole way.

"Sure there is."

I interpreted this a little ominously (was she planning on taking the car and disposing me somewhere?), and hesitantly asked why.

"We couldn't make it to Vancouver in this thing."

I know this car's a little shitty but –

"It doesn't matter. The road will be blocked."

Where?

"Don't know."

Then how do you know?

"Don't listen to the news? From what I've heard, everyone in Vancouver is trying to leave. Can't go south, can they? Americans won't let them. They've got ocean to their west and mountains going on forever to the north. So why haven't we passed any cars heading east?"

It was a good point. I kept quiet.

"I don't know where the roadblock is but you won't make it through in this car."

I became instantly anxious.

So how did you plan on getting there?

"I've got my own two legs haven't I? I brought a tent my family had in storage, and I've got some food. Hopefully that will do, and thankfully there's a flat road straight to Vancouver, not some dangerous trail. There's no room in my tent, if you were wondering. It's a one-woman tent."

I held a hand up. *Never would have dreamed of it.*

We were almost at the base of the mountains. They were immense, regal, like giant guardians of some dangerous land. I had to crane my neck forward to see their tops. I suddenly recalled the train trip of my childhood.

"If you don't want to go any farther, I would understand, but please drop me off as far west as you can."

Calm down.

We passed through the first pair of mountains and the road turned right. I kept my eyes forward. We had left the prairies.

"Do you always drive in silence?"

Hmm?

"Why isn't the radio turned on?"

Because I don't want it on.

"And why not?"

You're remarkably inquisitive.

"Yes."

Hmm. I thought in silence. *There's nothing the radio could tell me that I'd want to hear.*

"So you haven't heard the news today?"

No. Well yes. The Governor General is taking over.

She looked at me. Her eyes were light grey. Behind her, through the passenger window, a small lake hugged the road as it curved north.

I suppose you'll tell me.

She bit her lower lip and lifted her nose.

"The premiers of every province have announced that the Governor General's declaration of constitutional power is invalid. All but BC's met in Ottawa and released a statement, declaring that no unelected figure should govern Canada. They seemed to agree with the Governor General about security, though, since they indicated that they'd ask the military to help keep everyone safe. They went on to say that they will govern as a committee until free elections are held."

Shit.

"What?"

Nothing. Just shit.

"Indeed. Well they'll be meeting with the Governor General later today. Personally I think it's hogwash. It's right there in the constitution, why not let the King's representative guard us in a time of crisis. That's why he's there."

I suppose.

She stared at me.

What's America doing?

"They want no part of this. They're waiting until it sorts itself out, since they have their own problems. I thought you don't care about this."

Just then I pulled into an empty parking lot.

I don't.

"What are you doing?"

I pointed to a sign labeled: DEAD MAN'S FLAT – CAMPING GEAR.

I need some supplies, evidently. Want anything?

"I would like a tea. I will come in with you."

The man who owned the store was slowly packing everything away in his truck out back. He was closing shop. I bought a tent, some blankets, food, and other gear from him at an outrageous price, but I was desperate and he knew it. Little good my money would be soon, anyhow. Anne asked if the man had tea and looked pretty miffed when he laughed. He resumed his packing.

We got back in the car, and returned to the winding road out west.

*

Like most Christians, I questioned my faith in my teenage years. I accepted the weekly childhood trips to church, as part of the strange machinations of the adult world. I didn't question it. At some point, I started doubting the validity of church authority, and the existence of God. When you're a teenager everything is a battle, and everything is experienced for the first time through overpowering emotions. I rejected Christianity, and refused to go one Sunday. Alice dragged me along, literally by the ear, and I sat, infuriated with the rest of my family. When the congregation was bid to stand I sat. When they were called to take communion, still I sat. Stewart was embarrassed by my behaviour and told me so – the only time we've ever had a major disagreement. It was my one fling of rebellion, an unexplainable outburst of anger, and I stood fast.

That evening, Alice and I had our first and only fight. She yelled at me about my duty to go, and how I couldn't understand because I was so young. I don't remember what I yelled back, but yell I did. It took Alice off guard. I had never acted this way in our years at 45 Perkly. She stood over me with her hands on her hips. I was shaking. She walked away. Guilt swept through me, but I ignored it.

We never spoke of it again, but I was unofficially pardoned from attending church, joining Percy's ranks at home on Sundays. I began calling myself an atheist thereafter, refuting God whenever the topic was brought up. I can only imagine how annoying I was, young and arrogant, espousing my beliefs as if no one else had taken the time to carefully consider theirs. After awhile I calmed down about it, and called myself an agnostic. After all, how could anyone refute the possibility that God is there, somewhere? I essentially removed myself from the debate, and that's where my religious views stood for the better part of a decade. I cannot explain my volatile opinions on the subject, other than to chalk it up to both puberty and this: every Christian needs to question their faith at some point or another, and every Christian must do it in their own way. Agnosticism suited me perfectly. I was comforted by the logic behind it. However, with time my philosophy began to itch. It fit too perfectly. I was restless with how easy the concept was. I began feeling without, as if a gap was growing within me that needed to be filled. Years later, after I married, I returned to the Anglican community of my youth, and I attended church again regularly.

*

The winding road through the mountains was a stark contrast to the highway of the prairies. Through Manitoba, Saskatchewan, and Alberta, curves in the road were rare and the speed limits were cautionary at best. In the mountains, the road meandered its way north, then south, then north and south again, and it was often difficult to know what was a kilometer ahead of you. We drove wedged between imposing mountains, varying in shapes and sizes from grand symmetric works of beauty to lopsided, uncomfortable hills with exposed layers of earth. I felt claustrophobia nag at me. Four years in the prairies had made me accustomed to the open sky and the infinite land; here I felt fenced in, like I was being herded somewhere.

We followed the valleys and the rivers that allowed the road to be built in the first place, passing a rare car, probably leaving one of the timber or mining towns in the interior. When we did pass buildings, they were all empty. Anne and I spoke very little; I suppose we were both preoccupied with our own priorities.

By evening we reached Kamloops. Anne whispered "Wow," when we drove toward the lake. It was beautiful country. I recalled the sweeping forest fires that destroyed much of the region, years before. We agreed to pull into a motel at the edge of the lake. Neither of us wanted to drive at night, and we didn't know how far it would be until the roadblock. Better to leave in the early morning. We each took separate rooms. The minute I was alone I was inundated with anxiety again. I went to sleep.

*

This morning I had breakfast with Grace and Stewart. It has always been Grace's favourite meal ("It's like rewarding your stomach for being so patient. We're literally breaking a fast. Breakfast. Beautiful thing."), and today she took us to her regular restaurant, a hole in the wall down a street I'd never been to. I ordered eggs benedict, Grace the Big Breakfast, and Stewart the Early Bird Special. My dish was delightfully smothered in hollandaise sauce. The waitress kept the coffee coming.

"God this stuff's good," Grace sighed into her cup. "Sometimes I wish I'd never been introduced to coffee. Can't be good for me, the amount I drink." She said this as she poured maple syrup on her bacon strips and sausage links.

Sorry about that, I muttered through my toast.

"How do you mean?" said Stewart.

"Oh yeah!"

Yeah.

"Forgot about that."

"About what?" asked Stewart, who seemed a little put off to be left out of it.

"Our esteemed elder brother got me hooked. Thanks James," she gave me a sly wink.

"Tsk tsk, James," Stewart said as he bent back into cutting his bacon.

Sorry. I was young and foolish. Please forgive me. I gave a dramatic, slight bow.

"Oh you're forgiven," she replied with a wave of her hand, slurping her coffee with the other.

"So how'd you do it?" Stewart said to his plate.

Hmm?

"How'd you get her hooked?"

Oh. Well you remember how Grace used to piss off Alice?

"I did not!" Coffee sloshed over the rim of Grace's cup as she slammed it on the table. Stewart laughed at the exchange.

Yes you did.

"No way. I was a model child."

"Were not. Sorry Grace, but you were a handful, and Alice usually turned to James when you got to be too much."

Grace began to pout.

"But you're much more mature now."

"Jerk!"

Anyways, I said, glaring at Stewart. *When you were younger, like six or seven, Alice asked me to start taking you with me whenever I went downtown to study.*

"And here I thought that was out of the goodness of your heart. I remember that," Grace said.

"So you gave coffee to a toddler?" asked Stewart.

"No no, I didn't start drinking until my tweens."

"Much better," grumbled Stewart.

"More coffee?" the waitress asked. The conversation was put on hold as we all got refills.

No, at first she didn't drink coffee.

"Oh! The game!"

Yes, we played a game. Percy slipped us a bit of money before we left the house, for a snack. We'd get off at a different bus stop downtown every time, head in a different direction, and see how many blocks we could go without seeing a coffee shop. It was Vancouver. We were quite ambitious.

"That was the game?" said Stewart.

Yup.

"How many blocks did you usually go?"

"Oh, no more than five or six," Grace replied.

"And what was your reward based on?"

Finding the store. To pat ourselves on the back for whatever number we got, we'd go in and get a drink. After that we'd walk with our drinks to the library. She didn't start having coffee until just before you guys moved to Ontario. Before that it was hot chocolate. I guess you were trying to get the West Coast experience before moving?

She winked at me.

"And where was I in all this?" Stewart asked.

Don't know. You never felt like coming.

"Jerks," he glared at Grace, who stuck her tongue out at him.

Calm down everyone. It was a very long time ago.

"What did you guys do once you were at the library?"

Studied. Or at least I did. She usually coloured, or listened to music. For a while I think she wanted to be a flutist or something.

"Damn right," she said. "Chose the wrong career."

It was Stewart's turn to pay today. I usually want to take the cheque from him and pay myself: he's a stingy tipper. Can't tell any of us anything, though – we're all quite proud.

*

I woke up with the sun. My bed was larger than normal – this must have been a pretty good hotel – and I stretched my entire body out before getting up. I didn't know it, but that was the last night I would sleep in a bed for some time.

Anne's door was closed after I dressed, so I walked through the cold winter air to the lake's edge, and sat on a public bench to wait until she woke up. Not long afterwards, I heard a door shut, and turned to see her walking my direction. She sat down next to me, back straight, hands clasped on her legs. The wind whistled by us, making my nose and cheeks turn red. The water lapped quietly against the rocks.

Ever been here?

She shook her head. Her eyes surveyed the mountains around the lake, as if looking for some hint as to what was going to happen next.

She turned to me. "Are you ready to go?"

Yeah, I whispered. We walked back to the car.

*

By sixteen it dawned on me that Percy had an existence outside the walls of the house. I knew him very little beyond his role as a punching bag for Alice, and as a man who would occasionally give me a kind smile. I discovered that Percy was well loved by almost everyone he knew outside of the house; on his own, he had developed a community I was entirely unaware of.

At the request of my sister, I drove her to a party when she was eight. She invited me in, though we both knew I would say no. She was very kind; she knew I had few friends and she made great efforts to strengthen our own relationship. I turned her down and dropped her off. We were in Percy's battered truck, so she had some difficulty getting down from the seat – Alice had taken the family car to play bridge at Betsy's house. She always played somewhere else by that point. I helped Grace out and drove home, stopping for gas on the way.

The sun was setting as I walked into the gas station to pay the bill, and the man behind the counter winked at me and waved his hands in front of his face.

"No charge," he said. "You're Percy's boy, aren't you? Heard about you three. Recognize his truck. Your money's not good here."

I tried to protest, then nodded shyly. I didn't really know what to do in a situation like that, so I left. I drove home in his rattling truck.

Later, I mentioned it to Percy. He chuckled and said, "Yeah, Bill's a good guy."

*

The car never made it to the roadblock.

We had left the hotel just after dawn, and made considerable progress. We were coming towards the end of our drive through the mountains, maybe a few hours away from the entrance to the Fraser Valley. We rounded a corner and saw a family of four walking along the middle of the road. As I slowed down, I saw the children look to their father, and then to my incomprehension, spread out along the road, blocking my path. I slowed to a crawl. The father dropped his backpack and raised a rifle, pointing it straight at me through the front windshield. I stopped the car and raised my hands.

"Get out!" he shouted. I looked at Anne and we opened our doors immediately.

"Back away from the car."

I did so, as did Anne. The father motioned with his eyes to his wife and children, and they scurried into the car. The man continued to point the rifle at me.

"I'm sorry about this," he said.

I stayed quiet, motionless, breathing in the cold mountain air.

"Sir," said Anne, quietly.

The father was startled, and swung the gun towards her. His hands were shaking. She took a step back in surprise.

"Sir. I understand why you're doing this. There is a half a tank of gas in the car, which should take you well away from here."

I stared at her. The father's hands continued to shake as his eyes darted back and forth between us, rifle trained on her.

She continued. "We have some supplies in the car. We are trying to get to Vancouver. Please allow us to collect our things before you take the car."

He squinted at her, and I felt my heart pounding.

"Please. Otherwise we'll die in this weather."

After a moment he nodded. I reached under the front seat and pulled the lever to open the trunk. We collected our gear and supplies, dumping them on the side of the road. I opened the passenger door, hesitantly, since the father's gun was still pointed at us, and reached into the glove box to grab whatever money was left. The man saw this and said, "That won't do you much good".

Why not?

"It's a mess down the road, money won't help you."

Well just in case. I pocketed the wad of cash and joined Anne by the side of the road. The man walked slowly to the driver's door and stood for a moment.

"Sir," said Anne.

"Yes?"

"How far is the roadblock?"

He stared at her.

"Few miles back."

Anne nodded. The man got into my car and quickly put it in drive. Anne and I watched as he swung around and sped east. I took a deep breath and glanced at Anne. We looked to our supplies and sorted through them, trying to figure out how to proceed.

Alice is nearing her death. Since the cancer spread throughout her body, she's become incomprehensible, and has been kept under a watchful eye at the hospital. Her doctor agreed to let her spend the last of her days in her home, surrounded by family. The fact that a registered nurse and a retired doctor were among the family members helped in his decision, I'm sure.

Stewart and I picked her up from the hospital this morning, placing her delicately in the backseat with the help of a nurse. The whole way home she muttered and stared out the window, drooling from time to time. Neither my brother nor I understood what she was saying, except once.

"Where is that idiot?" she mumbled. "Who's he with now?" Stewart and I shared a quick glance. This was never a concern she voiced before. How can you measure the lucidity of comments from a woman in her state? We drove on.

Grace was at home, preparing to welcome her aunt once again into the house she'd lived in for the past few years. I knew she was a nervous wreck below her calm, professional demeanor: when it came to Alice, Grace tried to treat her like a normal patient. This is something I could never do, which is why I stayed off her case. I know Grace was relieved when Alice took a turn for the worse, and, like all of us, felt underlying guilt at that relief. Grace has played the caretaker for far too long in this family.

We got Alice set up in her own bed. She appeared bloated and strange. She stared straight up at the ceiling. Her hair was short. She's a far cry from the woman of strength we'd known her to be for most of our lives. Someone had thoughtfully put her favourite pearl earrings on her, but the effect was not reassuring. She had let go of this world, and it was as if those pearl earrings were the only small string tethering her to every day life. Grace catered to her, and made her as comfortable as possible. Stewart and I retired to the kitchen and made a pot of coffee, where Grace soon joined us. All we can do now is wait.

We've almost finished Percy's estate. We sold the home pretty quickly, for a decent price thanks to Stewart. I wonder how many days it will be until we start all over again with Alice.

The first day on foot, Anne and I walked until we found an area good enough to camp in. The night was coming on cold, very cold, but there was little wind and we were well layered. We found a small plateau above a quiet brook, and went about setting up our respective tents. Anne's was small, a one-person tent, and it didn't take her long to set up and sit on a rock to watch me. Later she told me that she hadn't expected me to know anything about camping, since I seemed the "quiet and timid" type, but was surprised when I set up my much larger, newer tent with little difficulty. We found some wood nearby and silently built a fire, then sat and stared at the flames as they licked along the damp wood.

After several minutes, I asked her where she was from.

She glanced at me, then back to the fire.

"Saskatoon."

Ah.

"What?"

Not much there.

"Nope."

She stared at the fire.

"Not much in Manitoba."

I grinned. *Good point.* I must have mentioned Winnipeg at some point. Maybe she saw my license plate.

You're far from home.

She sighed. "Yup."

Why?

She stared at me, as if sizing me up. "There's a boy."

Ah. Does this boy have a name?

"I don't care to talk about him. Why are you out here?"

There's a girl.

"Well then." She hunched forward and rubbed her arms.

Do you think we'll make it there?

"God willing."

Mm.

The fire crackled.

You're religious?

"Yes. Catholic. Are you?"

I haven't been to church in a long time.

"Never too late to go again."

Yeah.

She looked behind her.

"You did a good job with that tent."

Thank you. Yours is a little small. You might get pretty cold.

"I'll manage just fine thank you."

We kept quiet for a while after that, watching the fire. I guess neither of us knew how to deal with what we were doing.

"I'll say goodnight now."

With that Anne stood and went to her tent, leaving me to scatter the embers and head to mine for the night. I wished her a good night.

I slept restlessly. Anxious dreams flitted in and out of my consciousness, and in the middle of the night I woke abruptly. I left my tent to get some fresh air. Wrapped in all my clothes, I stared upwards at the stars on that cloudless night, the sky framed by the moonlit peaks of mountaintops. The still night felt eerie, surreal. There was no wind. I stared for a long time at the tall fir trees on the other side of the brook, and went back in. I had no idea what I was doing.

*

When I was sixteen, Percy woke me well before dawn. He gently placed his strong hand on my shoulder and whispered for me to wake up.

What time is it?

"Get up. It's time to wake up."

He left the room and I put on my slippers, then rubbed my eyes and stumbled to the bathroom. When I flushed and came out, Stewart and Grace were waiting for their turn.

I looked at Stewart. *Do you know what's going on?*

"I'unno," he muttered, and stumbled into the bathroom. Grace yawned and smacked her lips.

I walked into the dark living room and saw Percy bent over four large hiking backpacks, checking the smaller pockets. At the table, under a single illuminated light, sat Alice with both hands facing palm down on the wooden surface. She stared with a stony expression at Percy as he busied himself. I asked him what was going on.

"We're going camping."

Really? But it's Friday. We have school today.

"I already called your school and told them you're sick. Go change into hiking gear. There's clothing next to your bed."

I went back to my room to change. I was excited. Percy had never taken us with him, I had never been camping, and we had the day off school.

None of us knew what to say so we silently prepared as Percy instructed, under the eye of Alice, whose expression never wavered. When we were ready, the three of us lined the wall next to the front door like soldiers awaiting instructions. Percy looked at us quickly then walked past us.

"Well okay let's go," he muttered. Alice didn't say a word.

We didn't know where we were going but we didn't ask. This was so unorthodox and so exciting that we must have feared it would vanish with a whisper. So we remained quiet as Percy drove the cramped truck east. We were on the road for hours, winding through the mountains. By late afternoon, he pulled into an off-road under the heading "Lake Aldous." The truck came to a stop in an empty parking lot, and we stared with open mouths at the dark waters of the lake and the steep mountains surrounding it.

"I'll be right back," Percy said under his breath as he stepped out of the car and walked to a small store next to a long dock.

"Wow," my sister said.

"Yeah," my brother replied.

I grinned and stared at the lake ahead.

Percy returned and told us to follow him, ushering us out on the short, wooden dock and into a small motorboat. The paint on the side of it had long since flecked off. We stepped in bravely (we'd never been in a boat before, so it was brave for us). Soon we were speeding off along the shore, watching rocks and fir trees pass by in clusters.

It felt alien being on the water. I did my best to not think about how deep the water was, or how precarious the boat felt, thumping over the waves. I'd had swimming lessons before, but nothing to do with boats.

Percy pulled up to a solitary dock with a trail in the woods, and helped us out. I could see Grace about to complain, then stop herself. The boat rocked as we stepped out. The trail took an hour to complete, and ended with a clearing by the lakeside. My sister had blisters and my brother was tired, but none of us complained, staying silent for fear that this new development would suddenly end. Percy helped us pitch two tents, one for him and one for us, and then set up a fire.

We sat around the crackling flames until well past dusk. Percy spoke very little, listening instead to his niece and nephews talk idly of how lovely the surroundings were, and their teenage preoccupations.

During a lull in the conversation, Percy rose without warning and said, "Tomorrow we'll go on a hike. Um, make sure you put sand over the fire before you go to sleep. Goodnight." Then he went into his tent. Soon we heard snoring.

The three of us stayed up whispering into the night. At some point, as the fire had turned to pulsating embers, we threw dirt on it and stepped into our tent, falling into an exhausted, uncomfortable sleep.

When we woke at dawn I could hear Percy scuffling about around us. The sun warmed the tent so much that the three of us could no longer ignore the day, and we emerged, blinking in the sun. Percy wished us a gruff good morning, as he poked the fire under a pot of boiling water. For breakfast we had hot porridge and Earl Grey. I remember all the food that weekend tasting fantastic.

We hiked for an hour on packed down paths, ignoring the aches and pains of every steep climb. We came out from the woods onto a huge rock looking over the lake, the sun reflecting in a straight line towards us.

The lake bent around the mountain outside of our view. It was a magnificent sight, like something my wife would paint. We ate the delicious peanut butter and jam sandwiches that Percy took out of his backpack.

Grace looked at Percy when she was halfway through her sandwich. "Thank you Uncle Percy."

He looked at her without turning his head, and grunted his welcome through a full mouth. No one said anything else, and we headed back after twenty minutes.

Outside of our tents, Percy handed out chocolate granola bars, and told us we were going for a boat ride soon so we could return before sunset. We headed down, and Percy helped us into the boat and sped off. He took us along the unpopulated part of the lake, and we saw strange trees jutting impossibly out of sheer rock walls. The wind whipped through our hair, and the boat heaved up and down rapidly with every eave. My sister giggled, which made Percy laugh. The sun warmed us and we overcame our exhaustion with the exhilaration of speed. I'd never known such a feeling.

I dragged my hand over the edge of the boat to skim the water's surface, and Stewart emulated on the other side. He leaned over the side of the boat to watch his finger drag through the rapidly passing water.

"Faster!" Grace shrieked.

Percy turned on a dime while revving the engine. I watched my side of the boat lift out of the water, and laughed. I heard Stewart yell out. When I looked at him, he wasn't in the boat.

Percy! I shouted above the engine.

I recall seeing water thrash about in the wake of our boat. We didn't have life jackets on. Percy killed the engine, his eyes full of fear, and brought it back to life, returning to where my brother floated. Stewart flapped his hands about to stay above water. When we were close enough I jumped overboard and swam to him, pulling him towards the boat. With one swift motion, Percy pulled Stewart out of the water, and held his head between his hands as Stewart gasped for air. Grace helped me into the boat afterward.

Percy asked, "Are you okay?"

"Yeah," Stewart whispered, then coughed. Percy turned the engine back on, and sped towards the dock, while Grace hugged up next to Stewart. I sat and stared at all of them.

When we pulled up to the dock, Percy lifted Stewart in his arms, leaving me to tether the boat, and carried him the whole way to the camp. Stewart slept soundly in his corner of the tent, and Percy went immediately to his own tent after leaving sandwiches out for all of us. There was no fire that night.

We made our way back to the parking lot with the dawn, where Percy made a phone call from the store. He kept checking on Stewart, who muttered, "I'm fine, I'm fine." We drove back in a completely different kind of silence than when we arrived.

It was nightfall when the truck pulled into the driveway. I saw Alice looking out of the living room window as we pulled in. Almost asleep, we stumbled through the door, and Alice stared daggers at Percy. I slept the minute my head touched the pillow.

*

Anne woke with the dawn and began packing her things. The top of my tent grew bright. When she was finished disassembling her tent she walked by mine and declared crisply: "It is time to wake up." She sat on a stump and watched me bring the tent down.

How'd you sleep?

She stared at me.

Cold?

She continued to stare. I finished packing up and we headed for the road. It was impossible to tell where we were, but we knew we could not be more than two days from the entrance to the Fraser Valley. Beneath our feet the snow crunched clearly, and frosted trees stood quietly, watching us pass.

By the end of the day my feet were sore and Anne tried to hide her increasing stumbles. The sun sets early in the mountains, so we set up camp before dark. Her tent looked unimpressive next to mine.

You'll freeze to death in that.

"I'll be just fine."

No you won't. Come stay in mine. I promise to sleep as far away as possible.

Anne sighed and went looking for firewood.

We didn't stay long around the fire. We were exhausted from the road and had little to say. We went to our tents at the same time, and I wished her good night. I snuggled into my thick sleeping bag, and fell asleep.

After perhaps an hour, I heard someone clear their throat. I sat up and looked around. I heard it again, right outside my tent.

Hello?

"Hi. I assume your offer still stands?"

Yeah. Come on in.

Anne entered and promptly set up on the side of the tent. She tucked herself in and presented her back.

"Goodnight."

I smiled and rested my head on the pillow.

*

My wife and I were having a quiet dinner tonight. Between bites of roast chicken, she looked around her in surprise and asked, "Where's Theo?"

I looked at her with my mouth full. *He's at his place, hon. He's staying in with Jules and Rose tonight.*

She looked as if I had told her something absurd. Then she simply nodded and kept eating.

*

We woke sometime early in the morning. The sky lightened above us well before the sun appeared, and we shuffled to the road and started west. We weren't walking long when she began to speak.

"Do you have family?"

It took me a moment to respond. I wasn't used to her initiating conversation. *Yes.*

"Are they in the Vancouver area?"

No, no. They used to be. They're behind us now. They moved to Ontario five years ago. They live in a townhouse in Toronto.

"Tell me about them."

At first I was shy. I rarely speak about my family. I was also thrown off guard by her candid questioning. Thus far she had avoided conversations. Soon, however, I was telling her everything about Grace, Stewart, Alice, and Percy. It felt good to talk about them, and I realized how deeply I missed their company. She didn't ask about my parents.

What about you?

She took a deep breath and looked around her. "They too are behind us. My mother and father live in Saskatoon. That's where I started from before you picked me up. They didn't want me to go, but they know when I make up my mind."

We spoke most of the day. I learned about her family and her education – she had been training to be a teacher when she set out west. It was the most I had spoken in weeks, and it felt wonderful.

I was telling her a story about Percy when we rounded a turn in the road and stopped. Ahead of us was the roadblock. Two cars had collided head on and had spun, taking up the entire way. Behind, some cars had rammed into them, starting the logjam. And stretching down the road were cars in both lanes, facing us. From what we could tell, they were all empty.

"They must have all walked back."

I nodded. We weren't far from the Lower Mainland. Most people probably feared walking through the mountains in winter, opting for whatever there was back west. We began to walk along the cars, glancing into each one, looking for people. I was nervous: I felt as if someone was watching me. For the only time in my life, I wanted a gun.

When it became clear that all the cars had been abandoned, we headed off with renewed energy. We knew that we couldn't be far if so many people had given up and turned around.

It took us some time to find a suitable place to set up camp, and night had fallen when we walked down into a small meadow next to the road. As we walked farther into it, we noticed a fire lit, two hundred feet away. Anne headed there without asking, and I followed, hesitant.

The fire was being tended to by a man, woman, and child. The man stood suddenly when he heard us approach, and nervously demanded, "Who's there?"

Anne cleared her throat. "We're travelers heading for Vancouver," she replied politely, palms held outwards. "May we share your fire?"

"Vancouver? What the hell're you doing going there?"

Anne ignored the question. "You're heading east?"

"We're gonna try."

"May we join you at your fire for tonight?"

"How many are you?"

"Myself and a companion."

"If I say no?"

"We'll walk away."

The man hesitated. "Grab a seat," and with that he sat down. He glanced at the woman quickly.

We pulled up a large tree trunk and sat uncomfortably. We all exchanged names cordially.

"Listen," the man said, using both his hands to emphasize his words as he talked. "I don't like having you here, but I'm allowing it because there're some things I need to know. This is my wife and daughter. I will not hesitate to kill either of you if you threaten them. Understand?" Anne and I nodded. "We've decided to get out of here, even if we have to walk through the Rockies. Tell me about the road behind you."

Anne calmly let him know about the empty roads, where the roadblock was, the deserted towns along the way. He was relieved to hear that some places were still open in Kamloops. He listened intently, nodding with everything she said. When she was finished, he looked at her and said, "Thank you." She rubbed her thumb against the middle of her chest.

I cleared my throat. The man looked at me.

Excuse me sir. I just wanted to ask something. Why would you risk walking? What's happening in Vancouver?

He spit into the fire and glared at me. "Things got bad enough that we said fuck it, sorry, it's not worth staying here. Don't know why people aren't all walking, with the fucking, sorry, leaders pulling that shit? You heard about this?"

I shook my head.

"What's the last you heard?"

Governor General stepped aside to let the premiers govern. That's what she told me, anyhow. I nodded towards Anne.

"Ha! Fucking fat lot of good that did. Sorry, hon, but she's gonna have to get used to hearing me swear." His daughter smiled, embarrassed. His wife rolled her eyes. "Yesterday the premiers got together in person, to figure out how to put all this shit back together. Our man in BC wanted them to hurry, cause it's gettin' bad down there. Anyways, meeting starts, and they want to figure out rules for passing laws and decisions and whatnot, and those fuckers from Quebec and Alberta start babbling about their provinces being autonomous. They said that too much power in the committee would be a direct threat to their sovereignty – they didn't seem to like how many military men were walking around their province. Fucking traitors!"

80

He spit on the ground. His wife stared into the fire, and his daughter's eyes were trained on him.

"So they go on for another few hours and the Newfoundlander tells the fuckers to grow up, to help us. Alberta and Quebec start arguing that they won't sell their souls, and Quebec starts muttering about long knives. Oh yeah, they remember. Meanwhile, Ontario's trying to keep all this shit together when BC just up and walks out. He tells the camera as he goes: 'These clowns won't work together.' The GG threatened to take over again, unless they work something out by today. We haven't heard anything since. We've been walking."

Anne piped up. "How far until the Lower Mainland?"

"Not a day. You'll get there by tomorrow."

"Thank you," she replied. She sat back, relieved.

What's Vancouver like?

"It's not good. First everyone tried to leave, but you can't fucking go anywhere because the roads are all blocked, certainly can't go south, and the government is in enough fucking shambles that they can't help anyone. There was rioting after the Premier spoke to the cameras, and the grocery stores were looted a long time ago. Everyone fled, and now gangs are popping up that just wander around taking what they want. We needed to get her out, to hell with how hard it is." He looked at his daughter. She looked straight back, frightened.

Where will you go?

He shrugged. "Calgary."

Whatever's closest?

He nodded.

We stared at the fire for a long time. We each had our work cut out for us – we west, they east. I wondered how I would find Sarah in all that mess.

"I think I'll go to bed now," said Anne. "Thank you for sharing your fire with us. Good luck on your journey."

"You too. Thanks for the info."

I helped her set the tent up some ways away from theirs. She lay down immediately in the corner, and I went to mine. As I closed my eyes, she whispered, "Goodnight."

Night.

*

When I was seventeen, Percy and Alice had a fight. This in and of itself was remarkable, since normally Alice simply snapped at her husband, then he slumped away. This time was different. Percy wanted to move the family to Ontario. Stewart, Grace and I stood quietly in the hall in our pajamas, and listened to them yell at each other.

Percy started. "This is the only way!"

"Nonsense."

"How many years have I been telling you, warning you. We can't live in a house like this, I don't make enough money. Cutting corners isn't helping anymore. For a while, we could ride out the inheritance. But it's drying up. Out east, out east I can make double what I do now for half the cost of living."

"This is our home."

"Our home is beyond our means, you know that."

"We'll cut back."

"This is it, Alice. There are no jobs for me here. You can't work. I have an opportunity here, and I think we need to take it."

Silence. I never found out why she didn't work.

"What about the children?"

"They'll come with us. We can get everything out in six months, when the job starts."

"I'll be damned if I let you take them away in the middle of a school year."

Say what you will about Alice, but our education was always her first priority.

"Okay, then I'll go before everyone, get set up, then you can all follow when the school year's done."

Alice lowered her voice to a whisper. "This is our home."

"I know."

"My home."

"I know."

"And you're taking it away from me."

Percy paused. "Yes."

"Fine. We'll speak to them in the morning."

We snuck off to our beds, though I doubt any of us slept well. At breakfast they pulled us to the couches and stood before us. Alice spoke first.

"Your uncle has something to tell you."

Percy glanced at her before crouching to speak to us. "Guys, I've been offered a job. In Ontario. A friend of mine was just elected, and he wants to hire me to a very important position, as an engineer."

We were silent. Alice piped up.

"We will absolutely not leave until you've finished the school year." Her eyes fixed on mine. "This will give you the chance to graduate and decide for yourself what you want to do for university."

We all nodded. We'd had time to swallow this, and had little say in the decision. Grace sniffled a little, and Stewart's lower lip shook, but we accepted this sudden turn of events. Stewart and I still felt bound to not be a hindrance for Percy and Alice, and we didn't want to complain about the life they'd given us. I don't know why Grace took it so well. Maybe that's when she started growing up.

In hindsight I truly marvel at Alice. I don't know what drove her to protect us as she did. Maybe she wanted to help her brother's children, or maybe she wanted to prove that she could do what he couldn't. Or perhaps she simply loved us in her own way, and wanted what was best. Whatever it was, Percy kept his word, and I was on track to graduate with a high school diploma. We began the preparations for the move.

*

My eldest came for dinner last night with Jules. They left Rose with her other grandparents, so we were able to enjoy a less chaotic meal. We shared a bottle of wine and ate Chinese take out - an odd meal, certainly, but one we'd grown used to. During the meal, which we ate in the dining room, my wife rose suddenly, as if she had to be somewhere. There she would stay, look about, as if confused. I asked her where she was going, and she replied, "Nowhere," and then sat down again. This happened twice more. She was silent for most of the evening, playing with her food. Theo and Jules glanced at each other, notably nervous.

I awoke in the middle of the night and found the bed empty. I listened for noises in the bathroom, and when I heard none, I put on my slippers and went downstairs to look for her. The front door was open. I grabbed a jacket and ran outside, cursing. I took a right because it was closer to the intersection. As I stood near the stop sign, I saw my wife ambling down the sidewalk as if on a leisurely stroll, the light of the streetlamp casting her nightgown a pale yellow. It was cold – autumn is coming to an end. I ran to her and asked her why she was out in the middle of the road. She said Theodore and David were being mean to Brian again, so she took him out for a little walk to calm him down, and that he must have somehow gone home on his own.

I took her back to bed, and I didn't even try to fall asleep. This morning I drove her to the hospital, and that's where I am now, sitting in the waiting room. A gnawing, festering fear about my wife over these last few months has become a full-blown terror.

I cannot think of a more urgent time to write down everything that I can remember.

*

When Anne and I woke with the dawn, the family had left. We packed quickly and set off.

Neither of us spoke. We knew how close we were. We knew that this part of our journey was complete and that we were heading into a dangerous uncertainty.

By late afternoon we rounded another bend in the road, and the Fraser Valley opened before us. To the north a chain of mountains stretched west, framing the land I knew from childhood. To the south, Mount Baker stood as an imposing reminder that another country straddled this valley. And to the West, straight ahead of us, was a huge white tent. On top of it flew the flag of the Red Cross, and immediately around it were rows and rows of identical white tents, with scattered tents of different sizes and colours.

III

The wind whipped at us, cold and wet. We were just at the entrance of the Lower Mainland. My entire life I had never seen a refugee camp, and I was not prepared to witness this, not in Canada; I stood silent and shocked. Anne, perhaps because she was not staring at her home, or because she was far more sensible than I, recommended that we sit on a nearby rock.

I couldn't pry my eyes from the white tent. I had passed by this area before with Percy, but then it was empty fields and patches of farmland leading into the mountains. Now it was the beginnings of a refugee camp. For five days I had traveled across the country, wondering where Sarah might be, how I might find her, imagining what I'd say to her. In my thoughts Vancouver was continuously reliving the earthquake that I'd seen on television. It had been a constant physical disaster to me, and the aftermath could wait until I arrived. I never thought about where everyone would go. They left their shattered homes and fled to the mountains, and what they encountered was a city of tents, sprung up from the ground as donations from all over the world began to come in. Here they waited for the rains to stop and the mountain snow to clear before they could rebuild their lives somewhere else. I suddenly panicked at the thought of 45 Perkly buried under a landslide.

We agreed to walk towards the main tent, an hour away. Halfway there, we reached a checkpoint with armed soldiers, who let us pass after inspecting our bags. Along both sides of the road were small, family sized tents, laid out in rows. Between the makeshift homes, men and women were clad in thick winter jackets and dirty jeans, and spoke discreetly to one another. Children ran around them, playing games. Some people just sat on the side of the road and stared at us as we passed. Most looked shell-shocked, as if they were waiting for news they didn't anticipate would arrive. Some looked frightened and anxious. Some simply looked defeated.

It took some time to get to the large tent. Once there, we walked through the entrance facing the way we had come, on the east side. Inside it was bustling. Rows of gurneys and some equipment stations filled the area, though there were many open spaces, as if they were waiting for more supplies to come in. People walked about, carrying instruments and clipboards. It was a temporary hospital, with dozens of patients lying on their backs. I saw one doctor, hair disheveled, listening to the heartbeat of an elderly man on one of the nearer beds. Some areas in the corners were curtained off from view. Though the level of stress was certainly high, the system seemed well organized and mostly under control. There wasn't panic. We saw a sign nearby that stated: "Newcomers please register at the front desk – South Entrance." Instead of going through the hurly-burly, we walked out and around.

Behind the main tent, on its western side, we saw another large tent, though smaller, with a line of people that rounded out of view. I later learned that that was where the food supply was kept, and that it, along with the hospital, were the first two tents to be erected in the days afterward, with everything else coming quickly. In the eight days since the earthquake struck, this empty field had turned into an impromptu town. We walked through the south entrance and stood in line, waiting to speak to one of two women at the desk who were registering newcomers. From here they would send our information to a central location somewhere and cross-reference it with those registered as missing. When it was our turn, the younger woman asked us our names and where we were coming in from – she blinked at us and grunted when we answered Saskatoon and Winnipeg, respectively. If our presence as incoming travelers was a rarity, she hid her surprise well. She asked Anne her occupation.

"Teacher," she said.

"Teacher," the woman repeated, writing it down without looking up. "Would you be willing to volunteer while you're here?"

"Well yes, I suppose so, any chance to be of help. How will they reach me?"

The woman explained. "There's an information desk to your right, over there. Check in when you're ready, and offer your services. Do you two have a tent to use?"

I looked at Anne and she nodded without looking back. "No need to take up more resources than is needed," she told the woman with a curt nod.

"Good," the woman nodded, "we can use everything we can get right now." She turned to me. "Occupation?"

"Sorry," Anne interrupted. "Are you low on funds? It seems quite well set up now."

"Yeah, at first we were doing well. Lots of money came in after the earthquake. Came pouring in, really. Then after what happened in Ottawa, I don't know, I guess people don't want to donate to something so unstable. Plus, Americans are donating mostly to Seattle and that area, since they got some damage too. Money's still coming in, and we'll make do, but it's not as much as it was."

She looked to me again. "Occupation."

Oh, doctor.

She sat back. "No shit."

...yes.

"You're registered?"

Yes. In Manitoba.

"No harm in that. Hold on, please." She picked up a telephone and asked for a Dr. Beringer. "Thank you," she said to me. One minute later, a tall, lanky man in his forties strode forward. He seemed to cover a great distance very quickly without appearing hastened. When the woman introduced us, he turned to me with a warming smile, and asked if I'd be willing to help out. He had traces of a Newfoundland accent.

Yes, I replied without thinking. His personality was positively gravitational, and I couldn't think of a reason not to lend a hand. I needed to figure out what the next step was, and I thought that I might as well help while I planned.

"Excellent. Get set up and call me when you're ready to work. We're expectedly short staffed. Ha!" He slapped me on the back and walked away in long strides.

Anne came up behind me. "What a comical man," she said.

Yes.

When we finished registering, we received the information for where to set up our tent, and went to get started. We agreed that the left side was hers and the right side was mine, just as it was in the mountains. She began unpacking. I dropped off my hefty bag and returned to look for Dr. Beringer. Images of Sarah and my old home threatened to bombard my thoughts; I needed to stay busy.

*

Yesterday, after my wife's examination at the clinic, our doctor took me aside discreetly. I suppose he wanted an informal chat between physicians, but I was so filled with scalding anxiety that I could barely speak. He agreed that something is wrong, but before they start guessing he wants her to do some tests. He scheduled her in for tomorrow. I wanted to express my gratitude for whatever strings he pulled to make that happen, but I was fighting back nausea. Schedules at any doctor's office in Ontario are notoriously overbooked. I took her home and got her to take a nap in our bed.

*

The receptionist was right – internationally, money began to dry up. The Red Cross had enough to keep people alive and safe there until the end of winter, but not much beyond that. Despite this, it was a good place to be for Anne and I.

We settled in at the camp. I don't know what I had originally intended to do once I got to the Lower Mainland – perhaps search door-to-door, or wait patiently in Bean Around the World in the hopes that Sarah was of like mind. A much more efficient system was already in place. There was a section of the camp devoted to the search for missing individuals, and they kept a database of both those who were listed as missing, and those who had registered as alive with the Red Cross or any other agency. Anne and I both thought this a better use of our time, so we stayed where we would be close to information, in case either of us needed to act. We each registered a name under 'MISSING', and checked every morning to see if anything came up.

We ended up staying there for twelve weeks, from the end of January to the end of April, working and waiting for news. The affected area was so large, and the infrastructure so chaotic, we knew it was futile to do anything else but stay put. In the meantime we became occupied in helping out at the camp.

I started work under Dr. Beringer right away. It was an experience wholly unlike my clerkship or my brief experience at St. Boniface, and Dr. Beringer was unlike anyone I'd worked under before. His warmth and charm did not prevent him from running a difficult system in a stressful environment. I'd never worked in emergency care, and so it took me some time to adjust to the change of pace from family medicine. Some days it was quiet, and we calmly checked in on the patients who were there long term. Many had chronic illnesses and came to us when the hospitals lost resources and staff. Others had suffered injuries during the riots, and couldn't travel due to their condition. Some days we had influxes of people sustaining injuries like knife or gunshot wounds. Some were malnourished or dehydrated families seeking shelter: they walked in, bewildered and frightened, took our care with gratitude, and settled into a tent nearby. From time to time we got overflow from an emergency camp to the west, closer to the downtown core, where rioting and violence were regular enough that it would fill the temporary hospital beyond capacity. These patients were often aggressive; few of the people left in the heart of the city were law-abiding.

The patients would tell me stories about what was happening in Vancouver, and this shaped my image of the city. A few spoke as if this entire situation would resolve itself very soon, but most spoke in a dazed voice, as though the very core of who they were had shattered. These were men and women who were used to believing in the goodness of people, and of the invincibility of a well-run government. These were people who were witnessing the complete collapse of a society. The longer I worked there, the more and more patients I received who thought that the situation was beyond repair.

They were justified in their fears. News from abroad came quite readily while we were there, whether welcome or not. We heard all the political wrangling in Ottawa. From that far away, it seemed like distant, muffled yammering. The committee had settled into an uncomfortable truce, and the provincial leaders worked well enough to survive as a committee, though dysfunctional. They had agreed, after a short time, to send money to Vancouver. The priorities were security, a stable source of food and safe drinking water, and the clearing of the highways. We saw little tangible difference in the camp from the funds, though perhaps it staved off the worst for a while. We heard reports that the roads were indeed beginning to be cleared, but there were so many abandoned cars that it would take months. They also decided to set up a subcommittee charged with investigating the attack on Parliament. No one ever claimed responsibility, and neither the original investigation nor the subcommittee were able to find who did it. Regardless, the security clampdown that followed triggered riots in Quebec, and kept an entire nation paranoid for quite some time, waiting for a promised election call.

Near our tent, a Christian organization had set up, offering a place to pray, as well as Sunday worship. As I recall it was non-denominational, though at the time I paid little attention to such things. Anne volunteered there on weekends, and during the week she helped out at the temporary school that the Red Cross had set up. She taught elementary. I never saw her at work, but she talked to me about it at length. I think it gave her something to work on, and maintained her sanity. We kept ourselves busy all day, and often spent the evening walking about the camp together; there was little else to do to entertain ourselves, so we explored the area thoroughly. After a while, many of the occupants from the surrounding tents recognized us individually, and we got to know those who lived near us. Sometimes we stopped and spoke with families sitting outside their tents. Anne always initiated it, much to my discomfort.

We heard harrowing stories. There was a woman who pulled out of her driveway as the earthquake struck, and watched her house collapse upon her husband and daughter. Neither survived. Others spoke of watching glass tumble onto the downtown streets like rain, impaling or crushing people before their eyes. An older man told us how his house was robbed in the days after the earthquake. He was home, and he could do nothing but watch three armed teenagers take all his possessions. The stories haunted my thoughts and made me consumed with concern for the city of my youth. I grew anxious.

It is perhaps for this reason that I began smoking, a habit that I kicked ten years ago, thanks to the urging of my sons. Dr. Beringer introduced me to it, as we often took breaks together and he smoked avidly. For a dedicated healer he treated his body poorly. When not on duty he could be found with a cigarette in his mouth and a glass of scotch in his hand. He was well read and well traveled, and had been with the Red Cross for over a decade. His stories were mythical. He loved to talk, and his wit would pass me by in an instant if I didn't keep up. We became fast friends – rather, he took me under his wing.

Dr. Beringer was an old hand in these environments. He initiated me into emergency care and told stories of extreme cases while he dressed minor cuts. He taught me that half the battle was providing solace for weary patients. We listened together to their stories. When I told him my frustration that I couldn't see Vancouver with my own eyes, he told me to be grateful: "We're safe now, son. That may not always be the case. We're safe, and our patients are safe. Be grateful."

And I tried to be, but I often found myself looking west, thinking about how close I was to the city, wondering where Sarah was, and what state my old home was in.

*

In my final year of high school I had some decisions to make. Alice, Percy, Grace, and Stewart were leaving for Ontario after the school year, and had left the door open for me to join them or stay in Vancouver. I was tempted by both offers. In Vancouver I had a place of stability, a beautiful city I had known and loved since our cab ride from the train station. I knew the place well but could know it better, and it felt like I'd be cutting a relationship short by moving then. Toronto presented a place to live with less aesthetic appeal, but more to discover in its eccentric design. And that's where my family would be. If I stayed in Vancouver, it would be the first time in my life that I would be without the protection of adults. The concept frightened me, but appealed to my independent nature. I was torn.

I decided to do a tour of the two main university campuses in the area: the University of British Columbia, and Simon Fraser University. I knew I wanted to pursue the sciences, though I had no attachment to either establishment. I went to SFU for a tour first. I didn't tell Percy or Alice about it; if I was considering independence, I wanted to consider it independently. I took the bus from downtown Vancouver, which abruptly left the dense housing of Vancouver and began climbing Burnaby mountain; the SFU campus sits at its peak. Despite its grandiose location, I was not impressed. The entire campus was one grey, cement building, and despite the clear skies and shining sun, I felt depressed just looking at my colourless surroundings. I couldn't imagine how bad it would be on a cloudy day, which would be often on top of a mountain next to Vancouver. Still, the view of my beautiful city was magnificent. I finished the tour and waited for a bus.

I arrived at the UBC campus on the B-Line, a bus I would grow very familiar with over the coming years. From the moment I stepped off, the difference between campuses was tangible. The architecture was strange– one of the first buildings I saw looked like a giant concrete waffle – but the open space and the greenery were gorgeous. UBC had a beautiful campus, and they knew how to flaunt it. The tour guide, a third-year student, emphasized the scenery on his tour. The first stop was a simple balcony on the edge of campus, with a magnificent view. In the foreground, a carefully tended rose garden lay below us, while in the background there was the expansive ocean and a graceful line of mountains. It was an impeccable gem. How could I pass up living in this city, when I had four years of exploring ahead of me? I spent the afternoon seeing buildings and gardens that I would know quite well as a student.

I later learned that UBC spared no expense in how it presented its campus to the world. I still don't care; it was a beautiful place.

*

April let summer creep in early at the Red Cross camp, and the overcast sky was replaced with consistent sun. Anne and I both worked diligently at our respective jobs, spending our days helping out around the camp, and our nights strolling about. We knew the camp by memory, soon enough. I heard nothing about Sarah, nor did Anne hear about the man that she searched for. Neither of us spoke about them; indeed, neither of us knew the others' name. It was simply not something we discussed, and I never inquired. For me, every time I said Sarah's name made it feel more likely that she was dead. I also felt like the friendship I had developed with Anne was based on constantly being in transit. We were traveling partners, and talking about the end goal of our respective journeys would jeopardize the illusory nature of our relationship. At least, that's what I told myself. I have no idea why she didn't talk about her search.

We checked with the registration every morning, and every morning they told us that nothing new had turned up, but perhaps the next day. The futility of asking was becoming apparent. If neither had registered with any agency by this point, it was likely they would not be found. Again, we never spoke about it. We just kept trying.

Anne and I grew close. We depended on each other's company to share stories from the day, and talk about whatever was on our minds. She was a rare individual, whose company I did not find intrusive, and with whom I felt comfortable speaking candidly.

I don't know why she didn't reach out to anyone else to make friends, and with the exception of Dr. Beringer, I didn't either. Our environment was intrinsically impermanent, and perhaps we did not want to invest in friendships that could disappear the next day. She finished at the school at the same time everyday, and would be in the tent when I finished working. She was always reading one of the books that floated around the camp (she read indiscriminately), and did not acknowledge my presence in the tent until she finished whatever chapter she was on. Once she put her book down, she would abruptly ask about my day. I always thought it a shame that she didn't need glasses; her brisk nature would be well served by slipping on or removing a pair of glasses at her convenience. We talked about our days until dinnertime, and then we walked about at a leisurely pace, heads down, talking some more.

The topic looming over everyone's head was the lack of progress in the city. The committee of Premiers passed another bill to send funds, but there just wasn't enough money in it. Not nearly enough. While their somewhat stabilized arrangement tempted optimism, the money didn't even scratch the surface of the problems plaguing what was left of the city. Vancouver was in ruins; you didn't need to be in the actual city to know. The infrastructure had completely collapsed, and the aid was only enough to feed the survivors. Surely money was needed to stabilize the area, but the decision to send so little money was perhaps the final gasp of air before letting Vancouver go under. It was a lethargic attempt at regaining control.

Meanwhile, people began leaving the province on foot, and in great numbers. We saw family after family stop by the camp for one night, then head out with hefty backpacks and defeated looks. The residents of Vancouver were leaving the only way left to them, and as summer approached, the road into the mountains was not so inhospitable.

*

My wife is sitting, slumped in front of a blank canvas in her studio, staring through it. I can't imagine the tempest inside her head. I sit and watch her but I don't want to break her train of thought. So I write.

We returned from the doctor's this morning.

Calmly and sympathetically, he sat us down in his office, and informed us what his observations revealed.

"Physical tests don't always confirm what we think is happening to her. But she is definitely showing signs of advanced Alzheimer's."

I had suspected this for some time now, but I could never utter it. I held her hand as our doctor informed us, and she stared straight ahead, eyes focused on something else. I asked him how far along he thought she was.

"It seems to be degenerating rapidly, from what you've told me," he responded. She was looking at one of the medical posters in the examination room. "These things can happen quite quickly. It's difficult to make predictions with Alzheimer's patients, but at the rate you're describing she may not have much time before it becomes debilitating." He looked from her to me. "Of course, we'll start her on some medication to slow the process, but she's losing dominion over her memory. I'm sorry. She's going to have more trouble remembering recent events."

I nodded and looked at her. She looked ahead.

"Needless to say, this will be a difficult time for both of you. Alzheimer's patients often get confused, angry even, because they can't contextualize the present."

Okay, I said. I wanted to get her home.

"Call me for anything, okay?"

Sure. I helped her out of the office.

In the car I asked her what she was thinking. She didn't respond, but bit her lip and raised her nose. I wasn't going to get anything. I drove through the slush on the streets and got her home.

She's begun painting now. Dark, angry swirls cover the canvas.

*

Summer came on strong at the camp by the end of April. The days were warmer and clouds were rare. I grew restless. I was overcome with a desire to see my old home, to see if it had survived the months since the earthquake. The camp was far on the outskirts of the Lower Mainland, and I felt as if I was wasting what might be my last opportunity to see 45 Perkly again in my lifetime, unless I found my way to north Vancouver. I had come so far and had stalled, so close, just to stay near a source of news. There was another, smaller camp closer to downtown, and I decided to put in a request for a transfer. I went to Dr. Beringer, who sat at his desk in his makeshift office, legs propped up. He was reading a patient chart when I came in and told him I planned to move. After a long pause in which he stared at me over the rim of his glasses, he warned me against it.

"You're doing good work here, son, and it's much more dangerous there. Stay here. Work here."

I've made up my mind. This is important to me.

He looked me over for a long time, scrutinizing me. Then he sighed, and rummaged through his cabinet. He removed a bottle of whiskey and two stout glasses. They clinked as he set them down on the desk

"Well, boy. If you're going to be going anyway. Good luck to you." We drank quietly. Finally he said, "Fine stuff, ha!" He walked out of the room.

I told Anne about my plans, and she nodded in agreement. She told me that she was wondering when I would come to this conclusion.

I asked her if she'd come with me.

"Of course," she said, with a sad smile.

I think by this point we'd both acknowledged that we might not find what we came looking for.

*

By October of my final year in high school, I decided that I wanted to stay in Vancouver and go to the University of British Columbia. I had grades that likely merited a scholarship, and I had already sent in my application. I wasn't ready to leave my city.

When I told the family about my decision to stay, Alice was happy for me. UBC was a fine school; it was a reflection of my academic accomplishments and her undying efforts to secure my education. She assured me that they would contribute to my monthly rent for whatever apartment I chose. Percy, whom I thought would be happy for me, was sullen and reserved. He simply muttered a "congratulations," and headed for his office. Stewart offered me a gruff good luck, and said he thought it was the right decision. Grace was openly mad at me, and stayed upset for weeks. To her, I was abandoning the family during a big change in their lives. She came around only when she made me promise to help them move into their new home, and visit often, after school started.

*

We headed west, again. Anne and I packed up our belongings in our backpacks, and registered our destination before we left. We each requested that the Red Cross contact our families back home to tell them about the move. After Anne said farewell to her students, and I shook the hand of Dr. Beringer, we caught a ride with an ambulance that was headed for Vancouver. We sat in the back and saw almost nothing along the ride. We could feel the ambulance sway back and forth as it weaved through obstacles.

The Red Cross had set up a tent in Queen Elizabeth Park – the same large, beautiful park high above the city that I had visited with Sarah – and once we arrived we registered immediately inside their tent. The operation there was designed for a smaller scale; this particular camp was meant to take emergencies and victims of violence, then encourage others to head to the larger, better equipped camp out east. The Red Cross had converted a nearby hotel into a temporary residence for staff and volunteers, where they sent Anne and I to drop off our stuff before returning to lend a hand.

It was a clear day. That summer, in fact, was notably short of rain. I could see a great deal of the city from our elevated position. Nearby, the streets had been cleared of debris and abandoned cars to keep the area accessible, but many of the houses in view had extensive damage. Windows were shattered, whether because of the earthquake or the looting. Fallen polls and heavy branches littered the ground, and everywhere everything was unkempt. There were no people to be seen. The staff at my new camp told me that the residents had either fled to the safer outskirts of the suburbs, or were part of the groups near downtown, lawless gangs and rioters who wreaked havoc from time to time. From a distance, downtown looked serene, though I was told that it was an illusion; many of the windows from the skyscrapers had fallen and shattered, and some of the buildings had collapsed in the earthquake. It was hard to tell, from where we stood.

*

My granddaughter came over tonight. Hallowe'en just passed and her sugar rushes have died down, and as is our tradition, we've begun decorating for Christmas. She helped me place wooden statues of Santa and a miniature crèche. This is the first Christmas where she fully understands that she is about to be showered with gifts – and is understandably excited. To be honest I did all of the work; she spent her time mesmerized by a snowglobe, shaking it and watching the white flecks fall on an Eiffel Tower. My wife bought that on our trip to Paris two years ago, when she saw it in a gift shop in Notre Dame. We haven't really gone anywhere since.

*

The time I spent at the new camp was far more stressful. Here the injuries had less to do with the anxiety of trying to escape a disaster zone, and more to do with the violence of an imploding society with no police: knife wounds, gun shot wounds, and rapes were most common. I have no doubt that my time at that camp made me more cynical for the rest of my life, and I do not wish to dwell on the injustices I witnessed there.

From time to time I joined ambulances heading to the downtown areas, as part of emergency recovery efforts. Every time this happened, we were accompanied by heavily armed security, and for good reason. It was not safe at all. It was during these trips that I first saw the extent of the damage done. My entire youth I knew Vancouver well, where the poorest and more dangerous sections of the city were, and what they looked like. On my trips into downtown after the earthquake, the entire area now looked like a slum, prone to outbursts of large-scale violence. No one controlled the downtown core.

The drive down revealed what I had wanted to see but hated once I saw. Buildings were crumbling and badly damaged, and the debris of broken glass, looted goods, and garbage littered the streets, offering little access to vehicles. We passed through Main and Broadway, my old neighbourhood, and found burnt wreckage where businesses once stood, and graffiti plastering windows everywhere. Bean Around the World was destroyed, its front windows smashed open and its contents spewed onto the sidewalk.

I saw what remained of my beloved Central Library. The imposing structure that had stood tall, like a modern Coliseum, had burnt to rubble. Only pillars of smoked concrete jutted from the dark heap now, the blackened remains of centuries of knowledge. My own personal sanctuary. The last place I saw Sarah. Everywhere, buildings had been damaged by either the earthquake or the aftermath, turning this once proudly beautiful city to shambles.

I worked hard at the camp and felt my spirits wane. Anne and I shared a room with separate beds, and I found her continuing presence my only comfort. Speaking to her was like breathing life into my weary and furious soul. It kept me sane. She volunteered at a nearby Pentecostal church with a single staff member, the priest, and helped anyone who came through their doors. I joined her for worship on Sundays. It was solace in an environment swirling with anger and chaos.

In a fitting tribute to the remnants of Canadian bureaucracy, I was not permitted to smoke the entire time I was there. It was far too dangerous, they said, especially in a park, while Vancouver is in its dry season. A city crumbles around them and I am barred from one of my few sources of relief. It did not help my anxiety.

*

Alice passed away in her sleep last night. Grace called me in the morning to inform me, and we spoke at length about her. Grace was shaken, but relieved. I think she spoke for everyone. Alice's illness had drawn out a long time, and we wanted to be able to remember her as well as we could. She could be as mean as they come, and she drove us hard, but she took us under her wing when my father abandoned us. I am who I am because of her, and I feel nothing but gratitude to the woman I feared for so many years. The world has lost a titan of a woman. I'm glad that her pain has ceased.

I told my sister about our visit to the neurologist. She paused, and replied, "Well this is just a shitty time isn't it?"

Yes ma'am.

*

It was there, while we were in Queen Elizabeth Park, that the political situation in Canada destabilized. Money from the committee dried up completely, and provinces became increasingly reluctant to shoulder the huge financial burden of reversing Vancouver's fortunes. As the money stopped coming, accusations began to fly and the committee seemed to be on the verge of imploding. The Governor General was positioning himself to take over.

Rumours grew rampant in the camp. Word got around that America was quietly amassing troops at the border of British Columbia, and the Chinese began openly talking about retrieving the huge Chinese population in the Lower Mainland. It was difficult to confirm anything at the time, and misinformation spread quickly. The managers of the refugee camp became more and more anxious, and we all felt as if something dangerous was about to happen. I wondered about the state of 45 Perkly again. I also wondered how long it would be until I accepted that Sarah was dead.

*

We were weeks away from my graduation, and Alice and Percy had surprised me by securing an apartment for me. A friend of theirs was the landowner, it was brand new, and it would be ready by August. They paid the first three months' rent, and offered to pay half for the rest of my time there. I gladly accepted, and tried my best to familiarize myself with the area.

I walked up and down Main Street, noting with excitement the bus stops and grocery stores, and all the little nooks and crannies of this eclectic street. I passed several coffee stores, peering into each unique setting, before nearly passing by Bean Around the World. It was low-lit and long, sparsely populated, and well furnished with comfortable chairs. I ordered a tea and biscotti, and sat in the back, facing the front window. I was pleased.

*

Near the end of my time at the Red Cross camp, a patient came in whom I knew. It was the first time I recognized anyone. He was a friend of Sarah's, one of the people there the night I surprised her by flying in. His beard had grown untamed, and his clothes were tattered, but I recognized him immediately. He came in with a knife wound in his lower abdomen, and he remembered me the moment I began dressing the injury. I did not ask him how he got it because I valued the memory of cordiality between us; anyone still around by this point was likely a gang member.

His wound was superficial and I patched him up with little difficulty. I returned to his bed at the end of my shift to check on him, and we chatted for some time about Vancouver before the quake. It felt good to speak with someone I knew: it was like our stories set up a temporary bubble around us, separating us from the present. We never knew each other well, but our conversation brought a moment of impermanent peace. As the conversation died down, I asked him whether or not he had seen or heard from Sarah.

He shook his head. "No, I'm sorry."

It's okay. Long shot anyways.

"She's missing?"

I nodded.

"How long?"

Since the earthquake.

"Shit. I'm sorry man. I didn't know you two were together."

We're not.

"Oh," he said, looking at me. "Well hopefully she's alright. Maybe she just didn't register with anyone or something."

Maybe, I said.

I patted him on the shoulder and said goodbye. I walked away to change before heading to the hotel.

Sadness swept through me. I had felt for some time now that I wouldn't find her, and though this didn't mean that she was dead for certain, my brush with something tangible from our past felt like a damning indictment against the possibility of her living. In that moment I gave up on ever finding her. I gave up, and felt a sudden release, a freedom for which I still feel ashamed. I knew that I could reasonably abandon my search for her; she should have turned up by now. I vacillated between the lightness of freedom, and the grief that I had finally allowed to wash over me. I didn't know how I should feel.

*

This morning we got a letter in the mail. Not for us, really, it was addressed to my wife. There was no return address, but the postage was distinctly Asian.

She read it quietly in the living room. I did the dishes. After a few minutes she walked in and leaned against the doorframe.

"Brian got married," she whispered.

My heart leapt in my throat, and I turned to look at her. She was grinning.

To whom?

"A woman he met in Beijing. Apparently they'd run into one another a few times when he was traveling, and then it just sparked. Her name is Mary."

I grinned, and turned back to the sink. I felt tears welling in my eyes.

*

The night afterwards, Anne and I went for our daily stroll. Our walks were far less exciting, as it were, in this smaller camp. We were restricted to the protected park, and were advised not to breach the secured streets surrounding it.

I was quiet that evening, and listened to Anne talk about her day. Never in my life had I found someone's company so comforting, and I was absorbed in every story she told me. Her voice was soft, and steady. For a time after she finished we were both silent, listening to the wind rustle the leaves, looking up at the patches of stars in the sky, or down at the pebbles on our path. By chance our swinging fingers brushed together. To my surprise and gratitude, Anne's pinky finger latched on, and soon our fingers were entwined. Shyness kept me from looking at her face, and I silently relished the excitement of so simple a touch. We didn't speak for the rest of the walk. My heart pounded.

As we reached the edge of the woods that lead to the camp, Anne stopped and pulled on me with her hand. I dared not let it go. She looked at me in the light of the moon, and I felt nervousness build within me. With her usual candour, she said,

"So when were you planning on kissing me?"

I leaned down and our lips met. It was as tender a kiss as I had ever experienced, and I held her hand even as we broke apart. We headed back for the hotel.

When we returned to our room, we went through the same bedtime routine that we always did, except that before I turned the lights out, we stared at each other from our respective beds, with wide grins on our faces.

*

She is slipping away. She'll go hours being completely present and sharp, as she always has been, and will suddenly lapse and not recall where she is, or what she was doing.

This morning I was out in the shed, searching through my store of seeds. I wanted to plan for this spring's garden. It's cold outside, the backyard is filled with snow, and I was wearing my overcoat and scarf. As I was bent over, my wife opened the shed door and asked if I had seen the dish soap. She was wearing slippers and a nightgown. I looked her up and down, and said it was either on or under the sink. She went inside. A few moments later she had come again and stood behind me in the shed doorway.

"Have you seen the soap anywhere?"

I looked at her, and put the seed packets down. *You just asked me that, hon.*

For a moment she just stared at me. Then her lower lip trembled, and she walked towards me. She folded into my arms and pounded my chest with her fist.

"I hate this," she whispered.

I know.

She turned and walked back inside. A few minutes later she asked me if I'd seen the soap. I walked in and calmly placed it in her hands, and kissed her cheek. I returned to the garden, and mourned for the woman my wife used to be.

*

The next two days with Anne, perhaps the happiest days of my life, passed quickly. I slipped out of work to see her whenever I could, and at night neither of us could contain our happiness. Our brief cocoon of heart-twisting kisses and caresses stopped suddenly, however, with the news that British Columbia was splitting from Canada.

In the camp we got reports in written faxes from the authorities at Red Cross. The entire staff listened as our boss, a nervous, chubby fellow, read the memo aloud. It was written by his superiors at the Red Cross.

"The Premier of British Columbia has announced that the province is seceding from Canada. He states that the committee of Premiers has been ineffective in helping the earthquake's victims, even after several months. Here is a statement from his office: 'In response to the worsening political situation in Canada, British Columbia is officially seceding as of midnight tonight, and has agreed to join the United States of America as its 51st State. This is in exchange for full financial assistance in securing our cities and repairing the infrastructure, as well as the relief of our provincial debt. In addition, the President has agreed to send immediate military assistance to help bring order to the area, and begin the reconstruction process that is so badly needed. We encourage everyone to remain calm during the transition. Our hearts go out to those who continue to suffer physical and emotional pain from this ongoing tragedy, as well as the families of the deceased.' Evidently, we will continue working here to benefit those who need our services in Vancouver, but we must prepare for this change in political systems. We will be releasing instructions soon to the camp managers, who will inform everyone else. Thank you for your patience, and please remain calm for the benefit of those we are caring for."

The camp was soon abustle. I left immediately to go find Anne. She was speaking with a young couple at the Church when I walked in. She smiled when she saw me, and affectionately kissed my cheek. She sensed something was wrong, though, when I took her outside. I told her the news. Her hands clasped over her open mouth as she listened, and she sat down on the steps of the Church entrance.

"I suppose this was inevitable," she said.

Maybe, I responded, distracted.

"What are we going to do?"

I stared at her. *I want to see my old home before the shit really starts to hit the fan. I don't know if I'll ever have a chance to see it again after this.*

She stared back, then nodded. "Okay."

I walked straight back to the camp, and requested transport by whatever means necessary to get to North Vancouver.

*

High school graduation came and went, and I was easily accepted to the Faculty of Science at UBC. True to her word, Alice kept the stress of moving away from the children until school finished, and then kicked it into high gear thereafter. I was, in a painful turn of events, nominated valedictorian because of my marks, and so stumbled through an awkward speech in front of hundreds of people. I was relieved to finish amid their kind applause.

When I met with the family after the ceremony, Percy tried to hide the fact that he had cried, and Alice fluttered about taking pictures, commanding us this way and that. Never had I seen them so animated and agreeable to one another. Stewart and Grace were smiling, hiding their boredom.

They took me outside to talk, and Alice gave me a gift. It was an ornately framed photo of the family, taken shortly after my brother, sister and I moved into the house. They told me how proud they were, and how they'd miss me in Ontario. Percy asked me what's next, and that's when I first told both of them that I intended to pursue medicine. They smiled and nodded.

*

I waited by the reception desk at the camp to confirm that I could catch a ride up to North Vancouver. By this point, the administration was in coping mode, as the staff adjusted to the news of BC's secession, and prepared for an onslaught of frightened individuals.

The sun was setting as we got word of the Canadian Government's response. The Governor General declared a state of emergency in Canada. He claimed that BC's secession was illegal without a referendum, and that he was taking control of the executive branch, as was his right. This sent everyone in the camp into an even greater nervous hustle, but it was far too late on the part of the Governor General. Soon after his announcement, the Premier of Quebec rejected the "undemocratic, dictatorial claim to power," and declared independence from Canada. Within the hour, Alberta followed, staking their autonomy.

The camp was a mad scramble as it became clear that Canada had begun breaking apart. Indeed, no one was sure if Canada still existed. No one could do anything except prepare for an inevitable riot in Vancouver. Meanwhile I kept pressing and was granted transport with Anne in a shuttle heading to a North Vancouver mall the next day at noon, scheduled to round up patients and those wishing to flee the area. I went back to the hotel and informed Anne, and we quietly packed our things before submitting to a sleepless rest.

*

My wife and I went to church this morning. I watched her as her lips prayed without sound. I wonder what she prayed for. I wonder at the turmoil in her heart.

*

We waited in the camp well before noon the next day, to wait for our transport north. Someone was clever enough to locate a television and drag it in, tuning it to the news station. We watched as we waited, and, before we left, the world had weighed in on BC's decision to join the US. Of most importance, China had declared the agreement illegal, and announced that they "will do whatever necessary to liberate the Chinese patriots who are stranded in British Columbia."

It should be noted that most of the Chinese immigrants at the time lived in or near Vancouver, so mentioning BC as a whole was setting a pretty broad target. There were plenty of reasons to declare all of British Columbia fair game to them, not least of all were the resources that could feed a hungry Chinese economy, if they decided to invade. As the news recounted the Chinese government's statement, they showed clips of American tanks crossing the Canadian border in the morning light. They would be in Vancouver by nightfall.

The shuttle came and we hopped on, accompanied by two security vehicles. They anticipated violence.

*

45 Perkly was filled with boxes. Alice had a strict schedule for packing, and maintained it rigorously. She made lists of what things to pack on what day, and who was in charge of what. It kept us busy, because Alice seemed to think that moving house was no excuse for untidiness, and so we cleaned as we packed. I think she wanted a full schedule to counteract her own sadness at leaving.

We were all kept so busy, in fact, that I didn't have much time to reflect until there was more cardboard than furniture. With a few weeks left before the move, I was alone in the house for a few hours. I tried to read, but I was restless. I ended up putting my book down and staring at the living room walls.

I got up and started touching everything. The table in the center of the room, the kitchen counter, the doorframes: everything remained clean and well maintained. There weren't the telltale signs of a family house – stains on the carpet, a dirty front entrance, notches on the wooden doorframes – but it was nonetheless imbued with the memories of my life. It was a far cry from the farm that I could barely remember. It was the structured protection of my youth, and I was leaving it. We were all leaving it. I tried to accept that these were the last days I would be inside 45 Perkly, but I couldn't put it into context. There was no other home for me. How could I never again come home?

*

To get to North Vancouver we had to drive through downtown to access the Lions Gate Bridge, or else take hours navigating an alternative route. Anne and I held hands in the shuttle behind the nervous bus driver. We passed by the train station, and I noted with whatever amusement I could muster that we were taking the same path I took when I first arrived in the city.

We drove down the Georgia viaduct. Everything was calm. We could see no one. The officer accompanying us checked his pistol. Around us the skyscrapers closed in, and loomed up out of sight above us. Glass and heaps of burnt garbage were strewn throughout the street, and the shuttle had to drive slowly to navigate around all of it.

Suddenly something shattered against the opposite side of the shuttle and exploded. Fire flashed against the windows and quickly turned to smoke. The driver floored it. Outside we heard screams, and through the blackened windows I saw a dozen people, with bandanas covering their faces, charge the shuttle. Two had flaming Molotov cocktails. They threw them after us and barely missed, rocking the shuttle with each explosion. Through our windows, I could see more come running out from a back alley, and one raised a crowbar and shattered the window next to Anne. She screamed and tried to jump over me. A hand reached in and grabbed her leg.

The officer stood and fired through the window into the crowd. Someone screamed and everyone scattered. My ears were ringing. Anne shook as I held her, and I helped her breathe deeply as we entered Stanley Park. The dangers of the city passed as we made our way through the forest. The officer asked if everyone was okay, and assured us that there was unlikely to be any resistance from here on – few people inhabited Stanley Park or the Lions Gate Bridge. I nodded and tried to calm Anne down.

*

I sent a message to Brian this afternoon. This is what I wrote.

Hello,

I know you asked me not to contact you, and I'm sorry for having to do it anyways. Should you choose to ignore this, or if it makes you angry, I'll understand. It's just that Christmas is a week away, and we haven't spoken for a long time. I thought I'd write to you.

Your mother tells me that you got hitched. I'm so proud of you, son.

Your mom's not well. I doubt she wanted to trouble you, but she's not well at all. She has Alzheimer's, and it's getting bad.

Please come home. We miss you, and we want to meet our daughter-in-law.

Ok. Thanks for reading this.

Dad.

I don't know if he'll respond. He's his mother's son.

*

The shuttle dropped us off several blocks from my old house. I shook the hands of the officer and the driver, as did Anne, who seemed to have recovered somewhat from the shock. We walked the rest of the way up the steep mountainside in the sunny late afternoon. From where we were, Vancouver again looked like a peaceful city, unbroken by the events of recent months. We walked until we turned down Perkly Road, and I stared for a while at the street sign. At the driveway I walked Anne up the steep gravel through the trees. It occurred to me only then that someone might still be in there. When we were in the clearing of the front yard, I stopped and looked at the house, and Anne came to lean her head on my shoulder. I had not seen the house in almost nine years, and little on the outside had changed. The grass was overgrown and the garden had not been tended. No car was in the driveway, and when I rang the doorbell, no one was home. I suppose it was abandoned like most other houses in the region, as the tenants fled to what was hopefully safety. Why no one had robbed it, I don't know.

I took Anne around the back of the house, and shattered the backdoor window to unlock it from the inside. Anne stayed quiet, and I suspect she disapproved. We clasped hands as we walked into the house.

The inside was different from my memory. A thin layer of dust covered a nicer, more elegant interior. Whoever moved in after us had style, and had the money to indulge themselves with fine furniture and appliances. I showed Anne the house, room by room. I told stories about my family: about Alice's poker nights, Percy's secret handshake, the places where Stewart and I played, the fights a young Grace had with Alice. I felt torn between the nostalgia of being home again, and the ache of seeing the changes made after we left.

After I finished the tour, I told Anne to relax at the kitchen table, and I went about finding what I interpreted to be the best wine in the house, and looked for food and candles. Sunset came and I lit the candles at the kitchen table, poured us each a glass of red wine, and served canned anchovies with stale crackers. We smiled at each other as we ate, and relished this first bite of civilized comfort we'd had since before we met one another. Our meager dinner felt like luxury. There was, unfortunately, nothing available for dessert. We finished, and, after dabbing her lips with a napkin, Anne took my hand and led me to the bedroom, a loving smile on her face.

We kissed and undressed each other, fingers fumbling. For a moment she stepped back to remove her shirt, and I saw that she had a beautiful black cross tattooed above her heart, which she touched delicately while I pulled my shirt over my head. I kissed her again, and we collapsed on the mattress. We made love that night for the first time, and we fell asleep in the comfort of a bed that wasn't ours, in a house that resonated in my heart.

*

Theodore came by for tea this evening, at his request. Mugs of steaming Earl Grey sat on the table before us, and we spoke about his daughter and his mother. I told him that I messaged Brian, to which he nodded and said it was a good idea. He seemed hesitant all night, as if something dreadful hid next in line behind everything he said. I asked him what was on his mind. He tapped his fingers on the table and avoided eye contact. He asked how the biography was coming along, and I informed him with some pride that it was nearing completion.

"Good, good," he said.

He then told me why he was visiting.

"The business trip I took last week. You know that I took the wife and kid, right? We spent a few days in Calgary, and I spoke at a conference."

Yes, I'm aware of this.

"While I spoke at the conference, Jules looked up where your dad might be living."

I stared at him. He went on.

"We'd spoken about it for awhile, Dad. We didn't tell you beforehand because we didn't know if we'd find him, and didn't want to trouble you. We found him, though. Dad, we wanted Rose to meet her great-grandfather before he passed away."

Theo moved his chair closer. "He's living in an old folks' home. He's senile, and pretty fragile. The nurses warned us that he's rarely coherent, but gentle, and they took us to his room for a visit. We talked to him for maybe, I don't know, fifteen minutes, Dad, and he was really out of it. He didn't seem to be clear about how many people were in the room, and he jumped from subject to subject without making sense.

"Suddenly, though, he sat up. You could tell something had changed, clicked in his head. He sat up straight, and looked around him, and at us. He looked me in the eye and said, 'Who are you?' I told him, "I'm your grandson, Teddy."

I kept very still, and my eyes trained on his.

"He kept staring at me. Barely blinked. Then his eyes started welling up. Then he said this, 'You're Jimmy's boy, aren't you? You're…and this is…is that my great-granddaughter?'

"I took Rose's hand, Dad, and walked her to where he sat, and I said, 'Rose, this is your great granddaddy. Say hi.' He took her in his arms and rocked her back and forth. He cried the whole time. Soon he asked Jules her name, and shook her hand when I took Rose back.

"After that he slumped again, and he seemed out of it. He started talking about random things, exactly the same stuff as when we walked in. He didn't recognize us. We said goodbye after that and walked out."

Silence fell between us. I could hear the grandfather clock nearby tick. I tried to hide that my hand was shaking when I sipped my tea. My son seemed to be waiting for me to speak.

Why didn't you tell me about this sooner?

He shrugged. "I didn't know how you'd respond, and Jules, she thought it would be important to tell you before you're done your book.

Thank you.

"Do you want to know where he is?"

No, thank you.

My son nodded, and helped me clear the table.

*

Something woke me up in the middle of the night, as I nestled against Anne's back. It was pitch black in the room, and it took me a moment to remember where I was. I had heard a sound somewhere far off. I kissed her softly on the neck and reluctantly left her side, putting on underwear. I walked cautiously through the hallway to the living room, and stared out into the darkness through the front window. The silhouette of the city was clear in the moonlight. The room was absolutely still. Then I heard what woke me up.

Gunfire.

Somewhere below us, in Vancouver, I could hear the rattle of automatic gunfire. I kept watching in the darkness, and saw flashes of light begin to pepper the landscape of the city. Anne walked up behind me, wrapped in the bed sheet, and asked me what was going on.

I don't know, I responded, and we watched and listened as the gunfire increased in sporadic starts and stops.

Suddenly an explosion lit up the sky, followed quickly by its booming sound that rattled our windows. It was large enough maybe to destroy a house, and it was in the distance. We watched as more explosions appeared throughout the city.

There's a battle going on, I whispered.

Anne slipped her arm through mine. I told her we were too far away to be in any danger, since we were separated by the Burrard Inlet.

Somewhere in the Vancouver mainland, the fire from one of the explosions grew quickly. It expanded in sudden leaps around it. Houses burned as we watched, and within half an hour the fire spread out of control, fed by the tinder of a dry summer. I watched the city I loved burn before me, and I could only stare in shock.

We stood watching the fire grow, and we did not speak. Anne brought me back to the bedroom and comforted me, kissing my forehead as tears made their way down the side of my face. I lay on my back, staring up at the ceiling. Through my sadness, another emotion surged; I knew I was in love with her, and it bubbled up my throat like an unstoppable force and overflowed past my lips. She whispered it back to me in the dead of the night. We made love again.

Afterwards we lay on our backs and stared into the darkness. I said nothing and thought of everything I had lost.

*

Percy spent much of the summer after my graduation away in Ontario, while we helped Alice pack. We were all stressed to be living under Alice's militant schedule, so when Percy returned to Vancouver for a full week, Stewart, Grace and I were much relieved to have him back. Really though, his presence changed little, except that he could help pack. The weekend before he left again, however, he took me on a surprise camping trip, what he thought of as a rite of passage before I became an adult. I don't know how he convinced Alice to permit it – perhaps he didn't – since we hadn't gone camping together since Stewart fell into the lake. For her part, Alice was silent.

We packed up his truck and pulled out of the driveway before the dawn. It was unlike the last camping trip, he informed me.

"This, uh, won't be like the last time, okay? Your um…your aunt wasn't too pleased with the stunt I pulled last time around, and um…well let's say this one's a little different…"

I could tell he was having trouble talking. *How so?*

"Well for starters I plan on talking more," he sighed, encouraged. "Now last time I didn't talk so much, and, well, um…well I guess I want you to learn something from this, you know, this time. So I want you to pay attention on the road this time, okay? We're heading to Lake Louise. Now, um… now it's a long drive, okay, so…so let's talk a bit along the way, okay?"

Okay, I told him, smiling out the window.

The trip was one of the most memorable events of my life. He told me about his new job out east ("bunch of bureaucracy, y'know?"), and I told him about my expectations for university and medical school. It was as if an unspoken agreement had taken place, acknowledging that we were indeed friends and that, as friends, two shy men had to learn to speak to one another.

Percy pulled up to Lake Louise several hours later and I was struck by the bright turquoise of the waters. The wind whipped heavily about us that day, and the lake with it churned out impressive waves. He took me through a trail that lasted a couple of hours, along the way pointing out different plants and animal tracks, and how they might be of use. When we set up camp, he taught me each step, from erecting a tent to starting a fire, to cleaning it all up. I felt that I was being initiated into

113

his private world, and that I was on hallowed ground. As night fell, we sat around the campfire and he shared stories with me about his camping experiences. I brought up the time he took us out.

That made Alice pretty mad, didn't it?

Percy barked a laugh.

"Yeah, I know. You gotta pick your battles, I guess, especially with that woman. Wasn't worth it in the end, I suppose."

Why not?

"Oh, well…well cause of Stewart."

I scoffed. *Percy, we still talk about that weekend. Might have been the best two or three days of our lives.*

Percy blushed and smiled into the fire. We sat quietly and listened to the fire crackle. Then Percy spoke.

"You three saved my life, you know."

I said nothing, too surprised to know how to respond to a statement like that. We sat quietly while Percy smiled to himself. Now, years later, I wish I could go back and ask him what he meant, to elaborate, to say anything at all. But all I did was sit quietly. Perhaps it was for the best; Percy never seemed more at ease to me than in that moment.

The fire sputtered in the silence around us, and the stars had long since come out before we wished one another good night. He scattered the embers and we retired to our own tents.

*

We left 45 Perkly with the dawn. A haze hung like a light fog, and the air smelled of smoke. We didn't have an immediate plan, but we both knew that our time out west was finished.

We walked for two hours to the only large-scale commune we could think of: the mall. Sure enough, a tent had been set up, accepting anyone who came that wanted to spirit away, and the Red Cross had apparently increased the staff there since British Columbia's secession. We waited in line to register for the transport out, wherever the destination was. I smoked my first cigarette in weeks, which was calming.

While waiting, we heard the latest rumours from those around us. Everyone claimed to know how the fire started: it was terrorists, it was the Chinese, it was the Americans, disgruntled federal employees; you name it. Now, of course, we know that it started from a skirmish between militant residents in the city and the incoming United States army, who hadn't expected much resistance. What we did learn in that line-up was facts from the rest of Canada, which people whispered like gossip. The Ontario government, in an effort to show their commitment to a united Canada, was accepting any British Columbian with proper identification as a permanent resident, and was wooing other provinces to stick with them. Nobody knew what was going to happen, but it was agreed upon that the end of that parking lot line-up was likely somewhere in Ontario.

In the coming weeks we would find out the fate of the rest of the country. In the west, Saskatchewan soon joined Alberta as a separate nation. Manitoba, meanwhile, took a great deal of time deciding what to do. Some say they played Alberta and Ontario off each other, though the Premier said she wanted to consult the public. In the end, Manitoba joined Saskatchewan and Alberta (who were later joined by the Yukon) to form the newly independent Western Canada. In the east, Newfoundland held a referendum and decided to become independent again, neighbouring the new country of Quebec. Only Prince Edward Island, Nova Scotia and New Brunswick, along with the Northwest Territories and Nunavut, stayed with Ontario. They maintained a now diminished Canada. At the time, though, we didn't know; at the time, I hardly cared. I wanted to see my family again.

When we got to the front of the line, we registered our names with a stressed young man at a computer. After he took my passport and typed up the information, he reacted to something on the screen with, "Oh!" He then quickly left his chair. He returned with a harried-looking woman in a suit, who shook my hand and ushered me into a makeshift office. I grabbed Anne's arm and pulled her with me. In the office she took the rest of my information, and I insisted she take Anne's. She offered us the next flight out to Toronto.

"Of course," she said, "we'll contact your immediate family of your whereabouts – they should be waiting for you on your arrival. We have a transport ready to take you and your partner to the airport within the hour."

I nodded without understanding, and thanked her. I didn't know why they were processing us faster than the others in line. A man escorted us out and took us to a large white van idling behind the tent. It was almost full and was waiting for two more passengers after us. Through the tinted window, I saw the same man walk to the front of a long line of people that stretched around the tent, and took the first two, walking them to the van. For whatever reason, we'd been placed ahead of everyone else.

We boarded a plane with surprising efficiency, and were soon in the air. Vancouver stretched out below us through a thin smoke cloud. Anne slept with her head on my shoulder and her hand in mine, and I stared out the window at a country trembling on the edge of dissolution.

When we landed and emerged into the waiting area, Grace sprinted past security and gave me a jumping hug, kissing me on the cheek. Photographers from the media were clicking somewhere nearby. I hugged everyone individually, and then introduced them to Anne. Each of them was surprised, but soon hugged her too. Within minutes she was loved by the family, with the exception of Alice. She pursed her lips when it was revealed that Anne was Catholic. To her credit, she never spoke ill of Anne, but they've always had an icy relationship. Percy and Grace were simply happy that I had found someone. Stewart was grinning like an idiot.

Percy told me that evening why I was fast-tracked out of Vancouver. When he heard that Ontario was accepting British Columbians, but that there would be quite a backlog, he pulled every favour he had with his government position and somehow had me flagged as a low-level diplomat, a political VIP for the Ontario government. For this reason I was given priority when my name came up in their database.

When I asked him how exactly he pulled a stunt like that, he simply shrugged and smiled.

*

My wife's having a good day, and has been feeling pretty animate. She wanted to leaf through this autobiography, and I let her. She read mostly the sections involving her.

"It's nice," she said. "You certainly take some liberties with the truth, though. Frankly some of it is hogwash."

Fantastic. She can't remember what she ate for breakfast but she can remember details decades old and point out when I'm wrong. She's been quiet since she read it. I can't imagine that, despite her support for me writing this, she didn't somehow fear some of the content.

I hear her whistling in the kitchen below, quite happily. I assume she has forgotten it already.

116

*

A few months later, Anne and I were engaged. She stayed with me at my family's place for a while after Vancouver, having taken a short trip to Saskatchewan to see her parents. For quite some time it was difficult to travel between provinces: the political situation meant that whole new relationships had to be established, and the availability of flights was rare. Still, after I proposed, we went to great lengths to secure a flight out west, and within two months we were on a plane headed for Saskatoon.

Anne was an only child. Her parents were kind, melancholic people, saturated with prairie common sense and work ethic. I got along well enough with her mother and father, though my shyness wasn't entirely welcome. I would always be the quiet man who took their daughter away.

Towards the end of our visit, I passed by her parents' bedroom and chanced to look in through the crack in the door. I saw Anne's mother whispering solemnly to her, holding an opened piece of mail for her to take. Anne took it with shaking hands, then I moved on as her mother left the room. I returned to the door, now shut, and heard her crying to herself. I feared to ask her its contents, though I suspect that I knew.

That night she was distant, and hardly made eye contact with me. When we woke, she was her usual self again. She has never mentioned the letter to me. In our many years of marriage, we have never once spoken about those we searched for in Vancouver.

*

In late August the family moved. We watched the movers load box after box into a huge van, close the back and head off on the road. We would see them again in a few days.

That night we ordered pizza and sat on a blanket in the living room, looking out the front window at the city we'd be leaving. The downtown skyscrapers glinted in the waning sunlight. The house seemed bare and alien, but its shape could not dispel the memories, nor the sense of familiarity, which several years of living instills. We left after sunset, and I watched the house through the rental car's back window until the trees obstructed it, then watched the city pass by as we headed to a hotel by the airport.

In the morning we boarded the plane and I watched most of Canada pass me by. It was the first time I had ever been on a plane. I saw my mountains, even more beautiful and majestic from the sky, stretch beyond sight. I saw the endless prairies and its patchwork fields beneath swaths of clouds. I saw the rich green forests of the Canadian Shield cradle seemingly tiny lakes, reflecting sun into my window. We landed in Toronto smoothly.

The new house was charming, quiet and unnoticeable in the Toronto suburbs, but it would never be home for me. The minute I walked through the front door after Percy and Alice, I knew that I would always be a guest in this place. It dawned on me then that I had no home, a feeling that would remain for the better part of a decade. I was entering a time in my life of impermanence, where I collected little, and dust rarely settled by the next time I moved.

I stuck around for about two weeks and helped the family unpack and sort their lives out. We went out for dinner on my last night there, so they could wish me, Stewart, and Grace luck in the upcoming school year. Grace was sullen for the whole night and the next morning. I kissed her on the cheek and told her I'd see her soon, and she put on a half-hearted smile for me. I gave Stewart a hug and he wished me luck. Alice and I hugged, and she held me longer than I expected. I suppose this was how she told me that she'd miss me. I shook Percy's hand and he winked at me. When I walked away, I felt paper in my hand, and I unraveled a $100 bill.

*

So this is it. It's Christmas Eve, the better part of a year since I started writing. This account was certainly not my entire life, but it was something that, it turns out, I needed to share. I feel...relieved.

In the years that followed our marriage, I found a steady and reliable partner in Anne, who made me a better man in every conceivable way, and raised three wonderful boys with me. I found solace in fatherhood, and I have a deep pride for every one of my sons. I can only pray that I did a good enough job raising them, and hope that this memoir serves them, and their children, with a glimpse of the formative years of my life.

I worked as a family doctor for the next three decades, and with honour helped create the New Canadian Constitution. I consulted on the section regarding the right to health. My position was attained largely in thanks to Percy's connections. He retired several years afterwards, and spent the end of his days camping and popping by to say hello. In his final years, he bought a cabin by Muskoka Lake and lived there permanently, leaving his Toronto home mostly unoccupied. Grace took up work as a nurse, and spent much of her time caring for Alice when she became ill, who moved in with Grace after much convincing by the three of us. Grace remained single for most of her life, and had no children, something I always found strange. Stewart married his lovely wife and started his own family of two children, and he and I have remained close after all these years. Anne returned to university once our youngest entered kindergarten, and has taught elementary school ever since.

She has good days and bad days. On her good days she is sharp and warm, and her no-nonsense edge hasn't dulled in the least. On her bad days she is confused and frustrated, often forgetting whom she's speaking to, even if it's her own children. I fear a time when she'll only have bad days, and I will no longer be able to talk with my wife.

I'm grateful to my son for encouraging me to write this. The process has been exhausting, but I feel relieved to be able to point at something and say to my grandchildren, *This is where I came from.* For whomever has read this, I hope it was enjoyable enough to entertain you, and that you have a more thorough image of who I am, or who I was. Thank you.

Epilogue

My dad was always a quiet man. I used to see him at the living room table, newspaper all messed up in front of him, reading the obituaries when I woke up in the morning. I would say to him, "Dad, how can you read that depressing crap?" He'd take this deep sigh, look at me over his glasses, and say that they're "actually quite lovely to read." I never got the fascination with death, but then, I never really understood him. I guess he probably felt the same way.

My older brothers once told me about this book. They knew dad had finished it, but that was about it. He shelved it after mom got really sick, and no one asked about it.

This has been a terrible year. Lousy. Dad had a heart attack, and fell down a flight of stairs in the basement. His caretaker was there at the time, and she took him to the hospital right away, but by then he was dead. Mom passed away pretty soon after dad. Three days after, actually. She'd had dementia pretty bad by the end of her life, and there's no way she was aware enough to comprehend it when I told her that dad was dead. Most people I speak to sigh and say something like: "That's too bad, but there's something poetic about it, you know? It's like *she knew.*" There's something romantic in the timing, for sure, but it didn't make sense to me until I talked to Uncle Stewart. He told me that when dad last met with mom's nurses, they gave her maybe a week to live. That afternoon he died. I guess he gave up after he knew she was near the end. Now that's romance.

So now we've had this estate to sort through, and we boys have been left to deal with it. I found this pile of papers wedged between history books, in my mom's old studio. My brothers agreed to let me read through it first. Dad and I didn't exactly get along until the last few years. It's not a period of my life that I'm proud of, so I had some catching up to do.

On the inside of the title page there was a sticky note. It read: "Please publish this upon my death, for the benefit of my children and theirs. –James Augustus." So we're going to do that. We thought about it, and agreed that having an epilogue would be, well, quite lovely. I volunteered.

Dad was quiet, but he was strong. He had a presence. His voice was soft but you'd never miss a word he said. He was calm and deliberate, fiercely competitive – family games of Scrabble were the stuff of legends – but he hated conflict. No matter what, he was a peace-at-all-costs kind of guy. I can only imagine how my absence hurt him. He was loved and respected in the community as a kind neighbour, in his church as a generous Christian, at work as a hard-working doctor, and within the family as a reliable father and grandfather. Even when he and I had trouble, I don't think I ever stopped respecting him.

Mom was a real dame. In many ways she was the opposite of dad. She was a spark plug. We used to sit around the dinner table and argue, everyone but dad. Usually we agreed really, but wanted to argue anyways, and oh did mom stoke the fire. She would prod us, push us, argue against us, all while dad tried to calm everyone the hell down. In a lot of ways she was a liberal. She was a great supporter of women's rights, the right to education, and the arts community. In other ways she was frustratingly conservative. She rarely wavered from her Christian values, and did so only once, supporting my big brother when he came out of the closet. You should have seen her go to bat for him. Give him a sour look and she was waving her finger right in your face. She was also a militant defender of English grammar and vocabulary. She was notorious for stopping people mid-sentence when they said *tuxedo*. She would touch their arm, smile, and say, "Oh dear, you must mean dinner jacket." My wife still cringes because when I first introduced her to mom and dad, my brothers and I conspired to steer the conversation, making her say "tuxedo". Even dad laughed.

They are survived by Dad's brother Stewart and sister Grace (who, by the way, wasn't single at all. Last year she introduced me to a man she had been with for decades but had told no one about. She's a strange, wonderful woman). Mom was an only child, and her parents passed away years ago.

I don't know what happened to Sarah. Before reading this story, I never knew she even existed. It's one of those quirks of life, that if she never met dad then he would never have met mom. I guess I'm grateful to her for that. A part of me hopes that she lived and led a full life. I don't know.

Mom's final years were difficult. In an odd way it was a blessing, because it helped Dad and I bury the hatchet. More than anything, I miss talking to her. I would give everything I own for a good argument with her again.

The message that prefaces this novel was a letter I found on a notepad, buried in James' desk. I don't know if dad wanted us to even read it, let alone publish it. My oldest brother, Ted, for the record, is against including it (he thinks it tarnishes his image), but I think it makes dad more human to me than any other part of this book. In the end, he was just as full of shit as anybody. I think if I'd known that earlier, we would have been much closer. As it stood, I always had trouble connecting with him.

My parents were great people, and they must have been proud of the children they raised. We are a testament to their love, their intelligence, and their unending patience. I miss them both. Their grandchildren will hold this book, and all of my dad's writings, as an invaluable account of their heritage. For my brothers and I, we mourn our parents, and hold these pages close to our hearts.

Acknowledgments

This book could not have been written without the support of several people close to me. Thanks to John Dunbar McLean for providing the catalyst for this story. I modeled many of the characters and events after elements of his unpublished autobiography (well worth the read), and *Losing Dominion* never would have gotten off the ground without his inspiration. Thanks to my mother and father for providing beautiful stories to enrich my novel, for supporting me through the entire process of writing, and for their blessing to bring stories from their own parents' lives into the book. Thanks to Jocelyn McLean for being the first to read the book in its earliest form, and for all the support you'll be giving me long after this book is finally published. Thanks to Fraser and Greg McLean for their continuing support as well. Thanks to Adena Brons and John Brennan. You two gave me exhaustive, detailed feedback, asking questions I never even thought of, and gave me the energy to propel this book into publication. Thanks to Allison Mander for her beautiful artwork that never made it to publication, and for being a pretty awesome gal. Thanks also to Lindsay Vermeulen, for all her hard and beautiful work on the cover and summary. Finally, thanks to Denise Sousa, for your unquestioning steadfastness, continuous love, and unwavering patience while I wrote. There's no way I could have written this without you.

The Author

Mark McLean is a teacher by profession. He was born in Ontario, raised in Manitoba, and went to university in British Columbia. He is currently traveling the world with his soon-to-be wife, Denise, and is working on a non-fiction book, interviewing people about how they view their parents. He is grateful to you for buying his book.

Please visit www.losingdominion.com for more information.

www.ingramcontent.com/pod-product-compliance
Lightning Source LLC
Chambersburg PA
CBHW031833170626
46807CB00004B/1449